TED STAUNTON

JUMP
CUT

ORCA BOOK PUBLISHERS

Library and Archives Canada Cataloguing in Publication

Staunton, Ted, 1956-
Jump cut / Ted Staunton.
(Seven (the series))

Issued also in an electronic format.
ISBN 978-1-55469-947-6

I. Title. II. Series: Seven the series
PS8587.T334J86 2012   jc813'.54   C2012-902621-2

First published in the United States, 2012
Library of Congress Control Number: 2012938225

Summary: Spencer, an aspiring filmmaker, takes a trip to Buffalo
to get a kiss from an aging movie star.

*Orca Book Publishers is dedicated to preserving the environment and has
printed this book on Forest Stewardship Council® certified paper.*

Orca Book Publishers gratefully acknowledges the support for its publishing
programs provided by the following agencies: the Government of Canada
through the Canada Book Fund and the Canada Council for the Arts,
and the Province of British Columbia through the BC Arts Council
and the Book Publishing Tax Credit.

Design by Teresa Bubela
Cover photography by Getty Images

ORCA BOOK PUBLISHERS
PO Box 5626, Stn. B
Victoria, BC Canada
V8R 6S4

ORCA BOOK PUBLISHERS
PO Box 468
Custer, WA USA
98240-0468

www.orcabook.com
Printed and bound in Canada.

15 14 13 12 • 5 4 3 2

In loving memory of my father,
Frederick William Staunton, and my grandfather,
William James Stewart; and for my son, Will Staunton.

R.I.P. greatest Grandpa EVER!

David McLean

Ann

Deborah

← our moms and aunts →

twins

DJ

Steve

Spencer

bros

everyone calls him

Bunny
~~Bernard~~

the youngest at 15

ERIC WALTERS

BETWEEN HEAVEN AND EARTH

climbing Mt. Kilimanjaro

Actually going to make it to Spain this summer!

JOHN WILSON

LOST CAUSE

TED STAUNTON

JUMP CUT

making movies in Buffalo

RICHARD SCRIMGER

INK ME

LOOSE in downtown Toronto

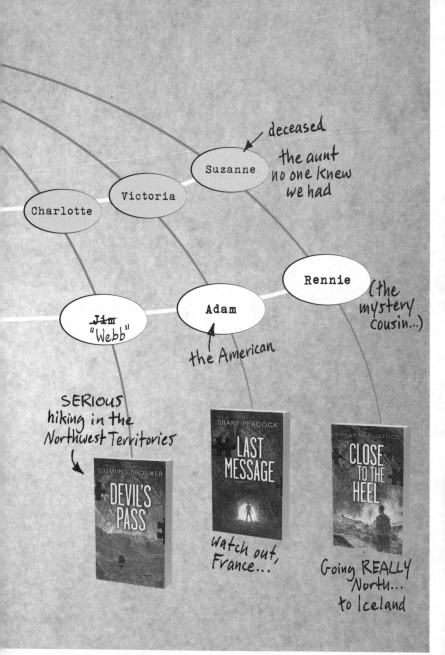

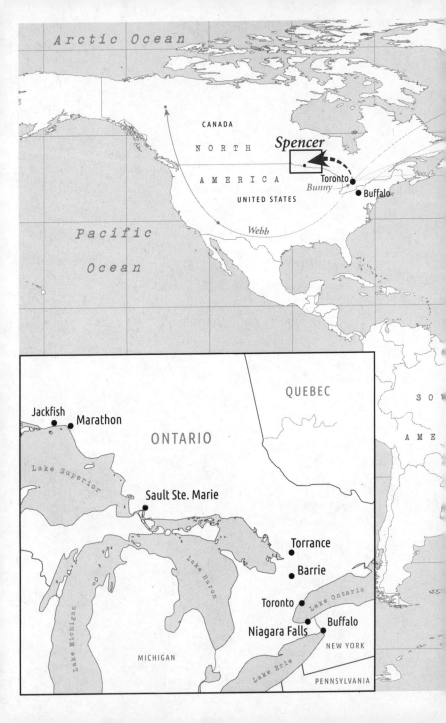

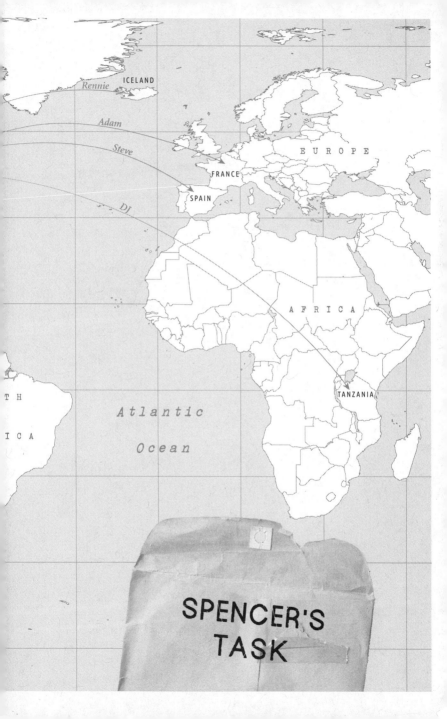

REEL ONE

"TWO SHOT"
BY SPENCER O'TOOLE

FADE IN:

EXT.–A COUNTRY ROAD–LONG SHOT, FROM ABOVE–DAY

A red Miata, top down, zooms along.

CLOSE-UP–SPENCER

SPENCER (Colin Farrell?) is behind the wheel. His hair blows in the wind. He's all in black with cool black shades. His chiseled face has a three-day beard.

EXT.—GATES OF HUGE MANSION—LONG SHOT, FROM
ABOVE—DAY

Miata turns in at gates of a huge mansion.

EXT.—STEPS OF MANSION—TRACKING SHOT FOLLOWS
FROM BEHIND SPENCER—DAY

SPENCER strides up steps to mansion. Door opens.
BUTLER nods.

INT.—MANSION HALLWAY—DAY

SPENCER walks down elegant hallway to giant doors.
He opens them.

INT.—MANSION LIBRARY—WIDE SHOT (SPENCER'S
POINT OF VIEW)—DAY

Two of Spencer's cousins, COUSIN DJ and COUSIN
STEVE, are arm wrestling while playing chess.
COUSIN ADAM flicks knives into a target across the
room. COUSIN WEBB hangs upside down, texting.
Spencer's brother BUNNY is on the couch, playing
with a tiger. BUNNY looks at SPENCER and nods.
The LAWYER sits at a big desk.

MEDIUM SHOT—LAWYER AT DESK

LAWYER

Spencer. Good, we can get started. Gentlemen…

WIDE SHOT—GROUP AROUND DESK

All sit around desk in leather chairs.

SPENCER

Sorry I'm late.

COUSIN DJ

(buttoning sleeve)

CIA again?

SPENCER

MI6.

COUSIN ADAM

(putting knives in pockets)

They always call me when I'm making dinner.

BUNNY

(stroking tiger)

It's nice to be wanted.

LAWYER

Ahem. Now then. Gentlemen, your grandfather's will is a curious affair. But then, he was a curious man.

All look up at painting of Grandpa in a massive, ornate gold frame.

PAN TO:
CLOSE-UP—PAINTING OF GRANDPA
GRANDPA is wearing a cool leather flying jacket and a black beret. He's holding a Colt .45 and a compass.

LAWYER (OFF SCREEN)

Perhaps I should let him explain…

SPECIAL EFFECTS:
Picture turns misty and swirls into a hologram. Pixels resolve into a 3-D GRANDPA. He's dressed all in black and now he's got a glass of whiskey and a cigar.

GRANDPA

Boys—sorry, men. I have a final mission for each of you.

ONE

Just kidding. I wish though. Really, we take the 501 Queen streetcar to the lawyer's office: Deb, Jerry, Bunny and me. Deb and Jer are my mom and dad. B-Man Bunny is my baby brother. His real name is Bernard. He's twice as thick as me and maybe forty-three times stronger. Bunster is your go-to guy for jars that need opening or cars that need to be lifted with one finger.

The lawyer's office is downtown. Don't ask me where; all the way there I was streaming *Kill Bill* on my cell phone. I've seen it fourteen times, but I like it. And I'm starting film studies in the fall at

Humber College, so it's important that I study the fine points—like Kiddo.

Also, it's better than listening to Deb and Jer. Deb is still uptight because Grandpa D was her dad and now he's dead. That's why we're going to see the lawyer. Deb insisted we dress up. Naturally that got Jer uptight too. Jer gets cranky when he has to take the bandanna off his head. Even Bunny knows that. Who knows why? It's not as if he doesn't have any hair. It's just that the front is creeping back toward his ponytail, which is something he really should lose, if you ask me. He hasn't asked.

Anyway, as we ride up in the elevator, Deb says to Jer, "You know how I feel about cowboy boots," and Bun tugs at his collar and says, "This scratches," and Jer hums "Ripple." I keep my earbuds in and turn up the volume.

All my cousins and aunts and one uncle are in the office. We find seats and the lawyer comes in and starts talking. I'm not paying much attention because Kiddo is really swinging her swords now. Next thing I know, everyone starts jabbering and the lawyer is yelling "Just stop!" or something, and a minute later all the parents get up and leave the room.

What's up? I don't know. I shut down my phone. Bunny moves over and sits beside me. "We're okay, right?" he says.

"We're cool, Bun. Whatever's going on can't be that big a deal. I mean, we're not the grown-ups, right?" I tuck my phone in my pocket.

It turns out there's something to watch anyway. It also turns out that I'm wrong about it not being a big deal. The lawyer messes with the remote for a flat-screen TV, and all of a sudden Grandpa D pops up on the screen, wearing his black beret.

The lighting is too bright. The colors are wild. Grandpa looks a little orange, as if he has makeup on. That alone would be pretty crazy. Grandpa D was not exactly what you'd call a makeup kind of guy. Jer always said he chewed rivets from his airplanes for mineral supplements. On the TV, Grandpa starts blabbing away about loving us all. It's kind of weird, seeing as how he's dead.

Bunny shakes my arm. "What's going on?"

"Ssh. We'll find out."

"What's Grandpa saying?"

"He loves you."

"I know that," Bunny says. "So?"

7

"Ssh."

Actually, it's a good question. No matter what Grandpa is saying in his video, I'm pretty sure he liked Bunny a lot more than he liked me. He'd start glowing anytime Bun wanted to wrestle or when he crushed a baseball out of the park. Comics and gaming? Nah, not so much. And Jer's "Front Porch Farmer" column for the *Parkdale Advertiser*? I don't think so.

Grandpa D was always after me to do manly stuff, although once he gave me a list of old movies he thought I should watch. That was nice, even though I'm not much of a black-and-white guy. I decide to look up the list when I get home, maybe watch a couple as my tribute to Grandpa.

Except now it sounds as if Grandpa has other plans for us. I listen more closely. Bunny is hissing at me again. "What's happening?"

"He wants us to do something."

"What?"

"We have to wait and see, Bun."

I shoot a quick look at my cousins. Bunny is a loud whisperer. They're cool with it though. They usually are. I don't have a lot in common with these guys, but they're good about Bun.

Video Grandpa tells us he has a task for each of us and then the movie is over. The lawyer is handing out large sealed brown envelopes to all us cousins. Now Bunny isn't the only one who's confused. We're all looking around, wondering, Whaaat? Do we open these now?

In a movie, this is where you'd cut to black.

TWO

In real life, Deb makes us wait until we get home
to open the envelopes.

Dear Spence,

Sorry I'm not there in person, but if you're reading
this, I'm airborne, as it were. Now Spence, I know
there have been times when we couldn't figure each
other out. I like to do things. You like to watch things.
That doesn't mean we can't meet in the middle. It's a
big place.

The middle has your brother in it. Watch out for him
always, Spence. Bernard thinks you're the bee's knees,

as we used to say, and he needs a co-pilot. I know you won't let him down.

The middle also, believe it or not, has movies. I like movies too. My all-time favorite movie star was Gloria Lorraine. Ask your mom if my liking Gloria L wasn't a family joke. Gloria Lorraine is older than me, Spence, but as I write this, she's still alive and kicking. I want you to go and see her—I know you can find her with the Internet and all—and get her to give you a kiss on the cheek. Tell her it's for me, a sentimental favor.

Film that kiss for me, Spence. Someone's got to make movies and this one only you can make. If Gloria Lorraine has passed or is incapacitated, look in the smaller envelope with this letter for your alternate movie mission.

The lawyer will have money for you to buy a good video camera and for travel and any other expenses you might have.

Make your first movie one that the family can watch and think of me.

Do these things for me. Do them with me. I know you can. Remember that list of movies I made for you? I hope you watched Casablanca. Remember what Rick says to Louis at the end? "This could be the beginning of a beautiful friendship."

Sometimes I'm a little too late to the station, but really, it's never too late.

Love,

Grandpa

THREE

Jer starts making pie dough while Bunny and I read our letters; he always bakes when he's bugged. At first, all the talk is about Bunny's task. Bun is supposed to get a tattoo of Grandpa's old fighter squadron logo from World War II. Deb is not big on tattoos, even if they are of Grandpa's squadron logo. "Oh please," she sighs. "The Marauding Mosquitoes? Their insignia was a mosquito with a cigar and a machine gun."

Jer shrugs. He's at the counter, rolling out pie crust. "Could be worse."

Deb shoots him a look.

Bunny just says, "Cool."

When they get to me, I hand over the letter and the other little envelope that's still sealed. Deb tears up a little when she reads the letter. I check my phone for texts. Then she laughs. "Gloria Lorraine. Oh, Lord."

"Gloria who?" says Bunny.

"That name rings a bell," Jer says. He's a trivia guy. "On TV…"

"*Cosmo's Castaways* and *Auntie Frank*," says Deb.

"Good for you." Jer's impressed. "Before my time, really, but I remember after-school reruns; well, *Castaways* anyway."

Deb shoots him another look. "Required watching at our house, even though you never actually saw her on *Auntie Frank*. She was the voice of—"

"The talking bulldozer," Jer finishes for her.

Bun looks mystified. It's the right look.

"Grandpa said she was a movie star," I say.

"She was in movies before she did TV," Jer says.

I go online with my phone and search for Gloria Lorraine as Bunny peers over my shoulder. There are a lot of hits. I start with Wikipedia. Up pops a black-and-white photo of a platinum blond.

"She's pretty," Bunny says.

He's right; pretty, but not stellar. She looks smart though, smiling at the camera with one eyebrow raised a little, as if she's about to say, *I know things you wish you knew.*

"Whatcha got?" Jer asks. He's sprinkling flour on the rolling pin.

I read out:

"*Gloria Lorraine (born Gayle Leonard, September 16, 1922, in Topeka, Kansas) is an American film and television actress with some fifty-two screen credits, most dating from her heyday in the forties and fifties. She also had roles in two TV series in the 1960s. Her last movie appearance was in 1972's grindhouse non-classic* Drive-In Savages.

"*Lorraine was discovered in classic fashion in 1939, waiting tables in a luncheonette in Seattle, Washington, where her family had moved in 1928.*"

"Well, that can't be right," Deb cuts in. "Grandpa was born in 1920 and his letter says she's older than him."

I shrug and keep on reading.

"*First signed to Republic Pictures, she had small roles in westerns, including two with Roy Rogers before—*"

"My hero," Jer cries. Is he kidding?

Bunny asks it for me. "Who's Roy Rogers?"

"A cowboy actor," Jer says. "Guys my age thought he was cool."

I read on.

"—*before moving on to both Columbia and Warner Brothers studios. Typically she was cast as a younger sister or the heroine's best friend in a string of largely forgettable wartime dramas and mysteries. She came into her own briefly in the late forties and early fifties in several minor classics of film noir, including* Blond Trust, Shadow Street *and* Dead Letter Office, *with costars Fred MacMurdo, Richard Wildmark and Ryan Robert*...blah, blah, blah..."

I skip a bunch of boring stuff. "*Dropped by Warners in 1953, she worked frequently in live* TV. *In 1958 she appeared (regrettably) in* Swamp Creatures from Zorgon, *which has made several lists of all-time worst movies. In the early and mid sixties she played the wealthy widow on the NBC sitcom* Cosmo's Castaways *(two seasons) and voiced the role of the talking truck on* Auntie Frank *(one season)*."

"Wrong," says Jer. "It was a bulldozer."

Whatever. I finish up. "*Apart from* Savages, *in which she parodied her role of the homicidal secretary in*

Dead Letter Office, *she has been in retirement since then. Married four times, she has two daughters. A complete list of her films is below.*"

That's it. I look up.

"So that's who she was—is," Jer says, rolling away at his dough. "I always used to wonder why the credits for *Auntie Frank* called her 'Miss Gloria Lorraine,' as if she was a big deal we should all know about. But really she was a B-movie actress who never quite hit the big-time. How come your dad had a thing for her?"

Deb shakes her head, then rests it on her hand. "Who knows?" she sniffles. She's crying a little again when she says, "Maybe Spence will find out."

FOUR

"Don't you want to film this?" Jer asks.

"Film what?" I say. It's Friday, just a few days later. We're driving through some ho-hum suburb in Buffalo, New York, on our way to the Erie Estates Retirement Lodge. It's ten o'clock in the morning. I should be asleep. Instead, Jer is at the wheel of our rented car. I don't know what kind it is, something boxy and boring, but it's nicer than our beater minivan. Deb needed that to bring files home from work or something. "Grandpa said to film getting kissed on the cheek. That's what I'll do."

I look out the window. All the houses are way bigger than ours. We slept over in one of them, my cousin Adam's place. He and my Aunt Vicky were there. Uncle John was away. He's an airline pilot. Grandpa liked that.

Adam gets to go to France with his parents to do something for Grandpa. Cousin DJ is going to freaking *Africa*, and Steve is off to Spain. How do they rate? I get to go to Buffalo to get kissed on the cheek by a ninety-year-old.

That's right, Buffalo. I'd figured that for an old movie star, I'd at least get to go to LA or someplace cool. Wrong-o. It hadn't been tough finding out where Gloria Lorraine was. She was on Facebook, and when I'd messaged her, she'd said, *Come on down to Buffalo*. Oh, yippee. Watch me struggle to contain my excitement.

Even Bunny gets to do something better than me. He's getting his tattoo today. How cool is that? How easy is that? Grandpa found the tattoo place for him. He'll probably be showing his tatt off by lunch. At least the whole stupid thing is only going to take a day.

I flip my phone open to check for texts. I should send one to Bun, just to say hi. He likes that; I like doing it too. Besides, it's better than thinking about a ninety-year-old's smooch. As if he's reading my mind, Jer says, "You don't *have* to do this you know."

"I know." I glance in the backseat. The new Sony video camera is there, in its travel bag.

"Don't get me wrong," Jer says, "I think it's great that you're doing this in Grandpa's memory and all." He has his bandanna back on, and a pair of mirrored aviators, with his plaid shorts and Converse sneakers. It's been cool all spring; Jer's legs are still pale even though it's late June. I'm not wearing shorts. I don't wear shorts, ever. "But," Jer goes on, "I can see how this could all seem a little wonky, you know?"

"I *know*," I say. I push my glasses higher on my nose. "I'm cool with it. It'll take, like, five minutes. And I have to, right? Everybody else is doing theirs." But really, I'm not that cool with it.

"No, but see, that's what I mean," Jer says. "You don't *have* to just because—"

Sometimes Jer just can't let stuff go. He's wrong, of course; I do have to do this because everyone else is doing their task, and the whole family will know if I wimp out. Luckily, right then Jer gets sidetracked.

"*In one hundred yards, turn left onto Eriebreeze Avenue.*" It's the woman's voice from the GPS.

"Eriebreeze?" says Jer, suddenly all concerned. "Eriebreeze? Is that the right name? These things can be wrong, you know. Are you sure you programmed it right?"

"It's cool."

Jer thinks technology peaked at bicycles and analog sound. It's a good thing he didn't want to pedal to Buffalo. We slow and hang a left onto Eriebreeze. "*You have reached your destination.*"

Up ahead, on the right, is a big sign in a clump of trimmed-just-so bushes. *ERIE ESTATES LODGE,* it reads in big letters. Underneath, in smaller letters it says, *Retirement Residency at its Finest.*

We turn in the drive and roll along to the parking lot. Gloria Lorraine, ex-movie star and Grandpa's fave, lives here. It's time for my close-up.

FIVE

"I'll come in with you," Jer says as he turns off the car.

"No, it's okay." I want the kiss and a quick getaway; that's it. I can see Jer asking for an autograph or an in-depth interview about symbolism in *Cosmo's Castaways*. I climb out of the car and then grab the camera from the backseat. "And she said to come in on my own," I add.

Jer says, "How are you going to—?"

"I'm cool." I close the door fast and start across the parking lot.

"I'll be waiting," Jer calls out his window. "Call if you need Roy Rogers."

Actually I'm not cool, and it's not just the heat in the parking lot that's getting to me. Now that I'm at Erie Estates Lodge, this whole thing is creeping me out a little. What is a ninety-year-old doing on Facebook anyway? That's strange enough. When I sent her my message about my grandpa, David McLean, asking me to get a kiss on the cheek for him, she answered right back and told me to come down this morning. She doesn't know Grandpa from a hole in the ground, so how weird is that? I mean, does she get her jollies kissing teenage boys? I've heard about older women being cougars, but for me, Scarlett Johansson is an older woman. I'm just glad I haven't told Gloria about the filming. That might be *too* kinky. What did Grandpa D have against me anyhow? Have fun in Europe and Africa, guys, I thought. How did they get all the luck?

Erie Estates Lodge reminds me of a hotel we stayed in one time in Montreal, when we all went to a conference with Deb. It's got this big arch thing over the front doors and the lobby has sofas and chairs and a fake fireplace burning even though it's hot out.

Gloria Lorraine said to ask for her at reception, so I go to a big counter that's not so much like a hotel.

The woman behind the counter has her hair pulled back tight and she looks as strong as Bunny. She's wearing pink hospital scrubs.

"Miz Lorraine is on the patio." She points the way.

I get lost anyway and end up in a lounge or something where a big flat-screen TV is blaring a game show at top volume. The place smells like a mixture of perfume and pee, and it's filled with geezers and geezettes. Heads turn toward me. It's a panicky moment. First thing I think is, Call Jer.

"Who ya lookin' fow-ah?" A thousand-year-old man, with impossibly black hair and giant black-rimmed glasses, is growling at me. He's sitting on one of those walker thingies, dressed to kill in a red blazer and a green tie over a yellow shirt that hangs off his ropy neck. All of him shakes, including his voice.

I say, "Uh, Gloria Lorraine?"

"SPEAK UP!" says the thousand-year-old, even louder than the TV.

"GLORIA LORRAINE." Now I'm too loud. Get me out of here.

"MIZ LORRAINE." The old guy glares as if I stepped on his white shoes. "OUT ONNA PATIO." He jerks his shaky head to show the direction.

His shiny black hair slips around a little. "Givva my regahds." He turns to the TV and then back to me. His eyes narrow behind his glasses and he nods at my camera bag. "You packin'?"

"No," I say, "I'm not going anywhere." I walk out to the patio.

SIX

It's a patio: flowers and garden furniture, umbrellas over tables. At first I think no one is there, but then I see the top of a red straw hat peeking over the back of a chair. I smell cigarette smoke. A voice says, "Well, don't just stand there." The voice is a bad imitation of the one I heard when I watched part of *Dead Letter Office* last night. That one was kind of smoky and sexy; this one sounds as if Jer has been going at it with the paint scraper.

I walk around in front of the chair. A tiny old lady is perched in it. Under the red sun hat she's got enormous sunglasses, and the rest of her face

is makeup and wrinkles. Platinum blond hair—
it must be a wig—grazes the gigantic shoulders of
her white jacket. She's got one elbow on the arm
of the chair and a cigarette between her red finger-
nails. Silvery bracelets with blue stones droop down
her skinny arm and into the sleeve of her jacket.
Her head moves a little. I guess she's looking me over
from behind the glasses. I think about calling Jer again.

"You the one who wrote?" she croaks.

"Uh, yeah," I say. "Spencer O'Toole."

"How old are you?"

"Seventeen."

"What was your grandfather's name again?"

I feel as if I'm taking a test. I push up my glasses
again. "David McLean."

"You don't—never mind." She waves the words
away with her cigarette. Bracelets clank. "Why didn't
he come himself?"

"I don't know." I shrug. "Maybe because he died."

She sits up straighter at that and her lips bunch
up. "What'd your grandfather say about me?"

"Well, uh, nothing. He just said you were his
favorite actress and for me to get a kiss on the cheek
from you, for him."

"Just on the cheek?"

"Uh, yeah."

She laughs. It's another horrible paint-scraper sound that ends in a cough. "Probably all I'm good for these days anyway. I used to be pretty hot stuff, you know. Not a bombshell, but a looker. And none of that enhancement crap either. You ever see my movies?"

"Sure." I nod. It's kind of true. Like I said, I saw a clip from *Dead Letter* online. And I'm definitely putting *Swamp Creatures from Zorgon* on my list. Any movie on all those worst-movies-of-all-time lists has to be too cool to miss.

"All me," she says. "The real thing. They didn't even have to cap my teeth. And legs? To die for."

"Uh-huh." What else can I say? I notice her feet don't reach the ground. I wonder how long this is going to take, and how weird it's going to be. Talking boob jobs in a retirement home isn't really moving things along. Problem is, I don't know what to do to move them along. Kneel down, maybe? Before I can, she changes direction.

"And is that what I think it is?" She pokes her cigarette at the camera bag. She still hasn't smoked any of it.

"It's a video camera. My grandpa wanted me to film us—I mean you—giving me the kiss."

"What for?"

I shrug again. "So my family can watch it? And think of him?"

She snorts. "Sounds a little kinky if you ask me."

"I don't know," I say. I can hear my voice getting a little desperate. "He left me and all my cousins tasks to do. This is mine."

"The kiss or the movie?"

"Both. So, anyway, if I could just, uh…" I take a step forward.

Gloria Lorraine hoists one marked-on eyebrow over her sunglasses. "Hold your horses, Spunky."

"Spencer."

"Whatever. I'm not that kind of girl. First we've got things to do."

I stare at her. She says, "What, you think I kiss every kid that comes mooning around with a hard-luck story? You've gotta work for it."

She flicks away the cigarette and hoists herself forward and out of the chair. She's surprisingly fast for an old lady. "Get those bags," she orders. She slips her purse strap over her shoulder. Beside her chair are a straw beach bag that matches her hat and a plastic bag from some store. As I stare, she grabs a cane that was hooked over the arm of her chair and starts motoring across the patio.

What can I do? I pick up the bags. They're heavy. I follow her along a walkway that runs around the outside of Erie Estates Lodge.

"What are we doing?" I ask.

"Just running a few errands. Where's your car?"

"In the parking lot. Errands? I guess my dad could drive us, but—"

Gloria Lorraine stops dead and doesn't turn around. I have to hit the brakes so I don't run her over. "Your father's here?"

"Well, yeah. He's waiting in the car," I say to her back.

"Can't you drive?"

"Sure, I can drive. I just—"

"Your grandpa—his father?"

"No, my mom's. His dad—"

"Never mind," she snaps. She turns around and whips off her sunglasses and glares up at me. Her eyes are brown with little blue flecks, and right now they're hard enough to shrink my gonads. "I thought I told you to come by yourself."

"Well, I did. He waited in the car."

She hisses a word I can't believe she knows. "Now I see why your grandpa wanted you to have the camera: to prove that you can do something *right*." She turns away and lets out a few more F-bombs, then finally says, "All right, come on, come on."

We pass some bushes and come out at the front of the building. Across the parking lot I can see our rental car, facing away from us. The windows are down and I can hear that Jer's found a classic rock station on the radio. I say, "It's over there."

"Never mind," she says, looking somewhere else. A smile cracks her makeup. "We'll take mine."

SEVEN

A white Cadillac convertible, top down, sits in the shade of the front arch, engine running. "I forgot I asked them to bring it around," Gloria Lorraine says, hustling toward it. She's pretty spry for a wrinkly. "Come on."

The Cadillac has a red leather interior. The engine purrs. "You drive," she snaps, yanking on the passenger door handle. I dump the bags and camera in the backseat and get behind the wheel.

"Come on, come on," Gloria Lorraine says as I fumble with the seat belt. She doesn't bother with hers, and the warning signal keeps dinging away.

I put the car in drive and we roll into the sunlight. The Caddy's the size of a whale, but compared to our family van it's, well, a Cadillac. As we roll past the rental, I'm about to call out to Jer, but I see from the tilt of his bandannaed head that he's probably Z'd out behind his shades. Gloria Lorraine sees me looking and says, "That your father?" I nod. "Why is he pretending to be a teenager?"

I don't know what to say, so I go with, "Are we gonna be long? Because he'll worry if I don't call him."

"He doesn't look worried," Gloria Lorraine replies. "And we won't be long—unless you keep us crawling. Step on it! Turn right at the end of the driveway." She's leaning forward as if she's trying to push the car faster. Or maybe she's just falling over; it's hard to tell.

As I make the turn onto Eriebreeze, I hear yelling back at the Lodge. I'm too busy driving to check the mirror. Gloria Lorraine acts as if she doesn't hear. Maybe she doesn't. There's wind noise and I have to ask her twice where we're going, plus her seat belt alert is still dinging too.

"Thirty-one twelve Lackawanna," she yells, holding the red hat on with one hand.

"Where's that?'

"What?"

"WHERE'S THAT?"

"It's—oh, hell, I don't know. It's close. Don't you have one of those GBS's?"

"It's your car," I yell back.

"Oh. Yes. Well, look; there should be one. It's got everything else."

I scan the dash for a GPS. There it is. "I have to pull over to set it," I tell her.

"Just make it snappy."

I turn onto the next side street, pull over and punch in the address. The GPS fires up and feeds me instructions. It turns out we're only three blocks away. When we pull up at a big modern house, Gloria Lorraine fumbles a piece of paper out of her pocket. "You all have cell phones. Dial this for me."

The handwriting on the paper is shaky. I get out my phone and punch in the numbers. Gloria Lorraine waves for the phone as if she's ordering champagne. After a moment she barks, "AmberLea? It's Gran. Are you ready? Well, get up! We're here…What do you mean, where? *Here.* Look out the window." She nods to me. "Wave at the house."

We both wave. As we do, I hear a funny *thump* from somewhere behind us. I look back to see if the bags have fallen over, but they're still on the seat. Then the front door of the house opens and a girl appears. She looks about my age. She's wearing a faded pink T-shirt and pajama bottoms with what I think is a Winnie the Pooh pattern. It's hard to tell at this distance. She's also got total bedhead: her straw-colored hair sticks out all over the place. She stares at us, the phone still at her ear.

"Get dressed and get in the car," Gloria Lorraine barks to her. The girl doesn't move, just keeps staring. "Hurry up," Gloria Lorraine barks again. "We haven't got all day."

The girl's mouth opens, but nothing comes out.

"It's borrowed." Gloria Lorraine answers a question the girl hasn't asked.

I say, "I thought you said—"

"Clam up," she says, without looking at me. I hear another *thump*. She yells to the girl, "Where's the Flexus or whatever it is?"

"Mom took it," the girl says into the phone. I can hear her without it. "The Mercedes is in getting new tires. Today's her golf day."

"I know that," Gloria Lorraine snaps. "It was always her father's golf day too. With redheads." She rips out another surprising word, then, "So: no car."

"No." The girl shrugs. She bats at her bedhead hair. "I didn't know you wanted—and anyway, you know I can't—"

"Five minutes." Gloria Lorraine cuts her off. "On set in five minutes." The girl ducks back into the house. Gloria Lorraine shuts my phone, sticks it in her pocket and mutters to herself, "We'll damn well have to drive this one instead." She turns to me. "Get me my scarf. It's in the straw bag."

I find the silky yellow scarf at the top of the bag and pass it to her. She loops it under her chin, over her hat and over her shoulder. "There."

"Uh, can I have my phone back?" I ask as politely as I can. "I don't want to lose it, and I think I ought to call my dad."

"Listen, do you want this kiss or not? We'll only be a little while. Besides, CB DeMille, you're going to need someone to shoot our love scene. AmberLea can run the camera. And when you speak to me, call me Miss Lorraine. Got it?"

"Okay."

"Okay, what?"

I sigh. "Okay, Miss Lorraine."

"Better. If you turn out to be reliable, you can move up to calling me GL. We'll see."

Thump.

"Did you hear that, Miss Lorraine?"

"Hear what? If she's not out here in thirty seconds, start honking the horn."

"Never mind." Maybe I've gotten lucky and a wheel has fallen off. By now, I'm figuring this whole thing is kind of sketchy. If this isn't her car, whose is it? It's all making me nervous. If I was *watching* it, that might be different, especially if AmberLea was superhot and there were zombies…

EIGHT

"Now we're talking," says Gloria Lorraine. AmberLea is trudging down to the car in skinny jeans, a red-and-white-striped T and flip-flops. She is not superhot. There is not much up top and she's a teeny bit wide for skinnies, but she has a nice face and the bedhead has turned into smooth blond bangs. She has red sunglasses perched up there too.

"AmberLea, this is Spritzer."

"Spencer," I say.

"That's what I said."

AmberLea looks at me with wide, worried eyes. "Hey," I say. I hear a squeak in my voice. I'm not that great with girls, even though I'd like to be. I try to get tips from movies, but there don't seem to be many seventeen-year-old sex-god movie stars with glasses, braces and a minor acne problem.

"Hey," AmberLea says back. She tries about a one-sixteenth smile, but even that much is hard to do because she's sucking in her lower lip and her chin is tucked so far into her neck it's practically in back of her head. *Dubious* is the word, I think. She looks as if we're trying to sell her chocolate shoes.

"Hop in the back," Gloria Lorraine says. "Now."

AmberLea says, "GL, what's—?"

"You said you'd do something for me today. This is it. And we don't have much time. Skinner here—"

"*Spencer.*"

"That's what I said—is a busy man. His father is waiting for him. We need your help."

"But you know I can't—"

"I'll deal with it. Get in."

AmberLea sighs and climbs in back.

"Go." Gloria Lorraine raps on the dash.

"Where?"

"Amby, guide us. We need a drugstore and a grocery."

In the mirror I see AmberLea roll her eyes and do an even bigger bite-and-tuck. Then she says, "The Price Mart has both. Turn around."

I do a not very cool three-pointer that takes us up on the sidewalk a little. There's another *thump* from the back. "What's that noise?" AmberLea says. "Have we got a flat or something?" I want to catch her eye in the mirror and give her an *I wish I knew but I'm not in charge here* look, but I'm too busy missing a fire hydrant. By the time I look back, she's got her shades down.

AmberLea directs us to a big supermarket. All the way there, Gloria Lorraine tells me to hurry up. When we get there, she has me park in a far corner, by a Dumpster. She gives AmberLea cash from her purse, and a shopping list. "And make it snappy," she says. "It smells like hell around here."

It is pretty ripe. AmberLea and I get out of the car and start across the parking lot. It's even hotter here than in the parking lot at the Lodge. We don't look at each other. The automatic door lets us into air conditioning that doesn't make me feel one bit better. AmberLea grabs a cart and, still without looking at me, says, "So what's going on?"

"Um, well, I wish I knew." And I wish I was Johnny Depp too. "Your grandma said she would help me make this movie for my grandpa, but she said before I could make the movie we had to run some errands, and she got really mad when I told her my dad had driven me here, but her car was all ready to go, so we came to get you so you could film us. Sort of."

I don't think my speech helps. AmberLea's chin has now completely disappeared. I'm betting her eyes are wider than ever, but I can't tell because she still has her sunglasses on. I guess it runs in the family. She says, "I don't know what you're talking about, but I can tell you two things: it isn't her car, and she always gets what she wants."

"But," I say, "it was out front, with the engine running."

"People do that at the Lodge sometimes, when they're dropping someone off or picking them up."

"You mean—?"

"All I mean is, the faster we do this, the faster we get the car back and get this over with, the better. I'm, uh, not supposed to be out right now. What's on the list?"

We get the economy-size Dependables adult diapers, five bananas, a little cooler chest, a bag of ice, Vega-Thins crackers and a pack of Marlboros. AmberLea doesn't say a word. At the checkout, I take a shot at conversation. "Your grandma moves pretty fast for a smoker."

"She doesn't smoke them," AmberLea says, as we pick up the stuff. "She just likes to pose with them. Don't ask me why." We walk back out into the heat.

NINE

You can hear the thumping from quite a ways off. Gloria Lorraine is standing at the back of the Cadillac, waving us over. "Open the damn trunk." She pokes her cane at it like a sword. I dump the stuff I'm carrying into the backseat and go to find the release on the dash. Behind me, the thumping gets faster and harder. "All right, all right," Gloria Lorraine says. *Whack* goes the cane on the trunk lid. I find the button, pop the lid, then hustle back. You can see little dents in the metal from the cane. I swing the trunk open.

"Aghh!" I jump back. AmberLea gives a little shriek and drops the Dependables. Gloria Lorraine says, "Aw, for the luvva…"

There's a man in the trunk, bound and gagged. Beside him is a Chihuahua dog, also bound and gagged. The man is wearing the kind of preppy clothes with lots of stripes that movie dads wear when they go golfing. Jer and Deb don't golf, to put it mildly.

The man and the dog both blink in the light. Then their eyes go wide and they both start wriggling like crazy.

I'm frozen. I don't know what to do. "Help them," AmberLea says, and she reaches for the dog.

"Not so fast," says Gloria Lorraine. "Frisk him first."

"What?" I say.

"You heard me. Frisk him."

"GL," AmberLea says, "somebody's already tied him up. Why would—?"

"Because sometimes they're stupid, that's why. That's exactly what happened in *Shadow Street*, remember?"

"That was a movie," says AmberLea.

"What difference does that make? It still happened. Frisk him."

Let me tell you it is *so* not cool running your hands over a wriggling, sweaty fat guy and sticking your hands in his pockets, even when it turns out there's a gun and a cell phone in his back pockets. I tug out the gun and stand there, holding the thing with my fingertips, as if it's a used Dependable. I've never touched a gun before. I've never *seen* a gun before, except in movies. It's surprisingly light.

"See?" Gloria Lorraine says to me. "I thought you said you watched my movies. Give it here." She snaps her fingers.

I hand her the gun. The guy wriggles some more and turns even redder in the face. His eyes follow the gun. Gloria Lorraine handles it like a pro, flipping a little lever on the side back and forth with her thumb. It's pointed at the guy in the trunk, and probably at the gas tank of the car too. The guy in the trunk starts making a noise like a clogged vacuum cleaner. He's squirming so much the car starts to rock. Gloria Lorraine snorts. "It's just a toy. It's too light to be the real thing. I hefted a lot of pistols in my day. Watch."

She flicks the gun to one side and pulls the trigger. There's a dry *crack*, then a *whang* and a ricochet whine, just like in the movies. A dent magically appears in the side of the Dumpster and there's a neat little hole in the Cadillac's windshield. "I'll be damned," says Gloria Lorraine. "It *is* real. Well, Spanky, let's get him out of there. I'll keep you covered."

AmberLea has already untied the dog's legs. When she gets the muzzle thing off, it starts yapping like crazy. The big guy in the trunk is harder to deal with. I peel off the duct tape from his ankles and help him swing his legs out of the trunk. He scooches forward, arms and hands still tied behind his back. I reach in and rip the duct tape off his mouth. I don't see there's a mustache underneath until it's too late. Some of it comes off with the tape. When he stops squealing, he switches to gasping. AmberLea puts down the yapping dog and helps me haul the guy up. Underneath him are what looks like a small gas cylinder for a barbecue and some clear plastic bags, the five-pound size that Jer uses to buy flour and sugar at the bulk store. These are filled with white powder and taped shut. Maybe this guy likes to bake as much as Jer does.

46

After he stops yipping like the dog when I pull duct tape off his hairy arms, he says, "You ever gotta do that again, try cutting the tape. Then a guy can soak it off, ya know?" He touches what's left of his mustache. He stops glaring at me long enough to say to the dog, "Mistah Bones, you all right?"

AmberLea has put the dog in the backseat. Now it goes crazy, scrabbling up the upholstery to get to the guy. The guy can hardly move. His arms are stiff as boards and his hands look all swollen. "Hey, hey, Mistah Bonesy, how we, how we, how we?" He leans down and the dog starts licking his face. There's a big red patch around the guy's mouth where his mustache was.

"Enchanting," says Gloria Lorraine. "We have to go."

The guy stands up stiffly. "Yeah. Right. Me too." He looks around. "Thanks fa helpin'. Ya wanna give me the gun before there's an accident? You can probably catch a bus at the corner." He sticks out a puffy hand and takes a tottery step forward.

"Not so fast," says Gloria Lorraine, and she points the gun right at the guy's belly. It's a big target. "We need the car."

He stops dead. "What? That's my car!"

"I doubt it," she says. "But even if it is, I doubt you'll call the cops."

"Hey," says the guy, "I'm an honest businessman."

"In a pig's eye," says Gloria Lorraine. She nods at the trunk. "Next you're going to tell us that the nose candy in the plastic bags is icing sugar."

"Exactly right," says the guy. "I'm a baker. Really. Lookit." He fumbles a card out of a pocket and hands it to me. "Al Capoli, King of Cannoli. See that tank in there? Helium, so's we can do balloons for kiddies when we deliver a deluxe birthday cake." He grunts as he reaches in the trunk and pulls out a bag of balloons.

"Uh-huh," says Gloria Lorraine. "King of Cannoli, huh? I hope you bake better than you lie. Ever hear of Little Moe Chopsticks, Dragon of Dim Sum?"

Al shakes his head.

"My third husband," she says. "Nothing to do with you, AmberLea. Your grandpa was number four." Then, to Al, she says, "How about Rocco Wings?"

Al's whole head goes from leather-interior red to Cadillac white.

"Thought so." Gloria Lorraine smiles. "*He* knew Moe and he's a fan of mine. Now, you could get in my way and make him very angry, or you could

48

help me and have him owe you one. My guess is you wouldn't mind staying on the move with us a while, since someone clearly wants you gone. If not, we can just leave you here—with your 'icing sugar.' I'm sure someone can help you carry it to the bus."

Al Capoli, King of Cannoli, bites his lip. His eyes dart around. AmberLea and I stand there. I can't believe what's going on. AmberLea's chin has disappeared again, so maybe she can't either. Even the dog is quiet. Then Al looks up and his eyes flare, and all of a sudden he hits the pavement in a belly flop. Beyond the Dumpster, through the trees at the edge of the parking lot, I see a black suv with tinted windows roll by. It keeps going.

"You can stay here and keep your mouth shut," says Gloria Lorraine, "or you can come along and keep your mouth shut."

"Let's go," Al says, scrambling up and brushing himself off. "Fast."

As we get in, Gloria Lorraine says, "You must have baked some awful cupcakes."

TEN

We get in the car. "Put the top up," says Al.

"Not on your life," says the movie star in the front seat. "Here, put these on." She rummages in one of her bags and comes up with a blond wig just like the one she's wearing, and another scarf. "AmberLea, help him."

"*What?*" says Al.

Gloria Lorraine says, "You know, shooting a man is like straightening your stockings. A lady's not supposed to do it, but sometimes you have to."

He puts on the wig and kerchief.

"And these." She tosses him some big sunglasses. The whole thing looks pretty interesting with what's left of his mustache. Al slouches low in the seat.

"Let's go," says Gloria Lorraine.

That's when I remember. "I have to call my dad."

"Not now, Sparky."

"*Let's go*," says Al.

All at once I realize that I'm in the driver's seat. Literally. "No," I say. "I call or we don't go. Grandpa would want me to call." I don't know if the last part's true, but it's worth a shot. I wave my hand to make my point, and the car keys fly away into the Dumpster. Now everyone groans.

"Now what?" says AmberLea. "Maybe we should all just take a cab home."

"Mistah Bones," says Al, from under the wig and kerchief.

"What?"

"Mistah Bones. Put him in there. He finds my keys for me alla the time. Watch."

Al scoops up the Chihuahua, gets out of the car and hoists the dog to the top of the Dumpster. The dog goes crazy, all four legs pedaling as if he's on an imaginary bicycle. It probably smells like dog heaven to him. "Keys, Mistah Bones," croons Al. "Keys for Papa." Al lets go. The dog dives. There's a lot of yipping, thumping and scrabbling, then the sound of Mister Bones whining. "Told you," Al says proudly. "Get him out."

"Cell phone first," I say to Gloria Lorraine. She hands it to me. I climb up the side of the Dumpster. The smell makes my eyes water. Mister Bones is perched on a green bag, the keys in his mouth. I lift him out. The smell comes along. Everyone groans again as I put him in the backseat. I ignore them and punch in Jer's number. It's time to get out of this zoo.

"Yo." Jer sounds as if I woke him. "Spence. What's happening?"

"Well," I say, "I'm with Gl—Miss Lorraine."

"Cool. So, mission accomplished? You've been a while. I must have snoozed. You done soon?"

"Well, that's the thing." I know I have to be careful here. Gloria Lorraine still has the gun in her lap. "We're not exactly at the Lodge right now. We're, um, running some errands. Kind of. And it's going to take us a couple more hours—"

"Days," says Gloria Lorraine.

"Days," I say.

"DAYS?" That's me, Jer, Al and AmberLea all at once. Our voices go up like roller coasters.

Gloria Lorraine nods.

"Uh, yeah, days," I say to Jer.

"Or no kiss," says Gloria Lorraine.

"Or no kiss," I repeat. Oh yeah; for a moment I'd forgotten that. "I guess I have to."

"Listen, Spence." Jer's voice gets firmer. "No, you don't. This is screwy enough already. Tell me where you are and I'll come get you."

It sounds good to me. I look around. But what do I tell him? That I'm sitting near a supermarket, behind a Dumpster, in a white Caddy with a trunk full of something that probably isn't icing sugar. I'm with a grumpy girl, a sketchy baker, a stinky Chihuahua and a ninety-year-old with a loaded gun? Do I just say, *You'll know us when you see us*? For a second I wonder what Bunny would think of this. What will I tell him? I think of my cousins in France or Spain or Africa. What will I tell them? And AmberLea, who, while not superhot, is still pretty nice in skinny jeans: am I going to wimp out in front of her, just because her grandma waves a pistol with the safety off? What would I tell Grandpa? I think of how I dreamed of making my own movie. I take a deep breath. "No," I say, "it's okay. I'm cool with it. I have to make the movie."

Behind me, Al says, "Movie? Over my dead body."

"Obviously *that* can be arranged," says Gloria Lorraine. Mister Bones yelps.

"Was that a dog?" Jer asks.

"Yeah, we're at one of those dog-grooming places." Where did that come from? I don't know. All I know is that I've got to finish this. "Why don't you go back to Aunt Vicky's?"

"Tell him to go home," says Gloria Lorraine. "I'll get you back there."

"Or go home," I say to Jer. "Miss Lorraine promises to get me back."

"But—" Jer says.

"I've got to go."

"Damn right," Al says.

I ignore him. "A couple of days. I'll call. I promise. Nothing to worry about."

"But, Spence—"

"Trust me," I say. I switch off the phone. My heart is pounding, but it's a good pounding. I think.

"That's more like it," says Gloria Lorraine. "I bet that's what your grandpa would have done." She points to the GPS. "Now, aim that thing north and get us to Canada."

REEL TWO

EXT.—LONG SHOT—DAY

A white Cadillac convertible, top down, rolls slowly to a fortified border crossing on a country road: guard tower, machine guns, tank traps, sandbags topped with concertina wire. Armed sentries man the gate. As the Cadillac stops, a SOLDIER steps to driver's side. SPENCER is driving, AMBERLEA (Amy Faris?) in front passenger seat, GLORIA LORRAINE (Betty White) in backseat with MISTER BONES on lap.

EXT.–WIDE SHOT LOOKING UP TO SOLDIER FROM
SPENCER'S P.O.V.–DAY

                    SOLDIER
           (snapping fingers twice)
     Papers. Passports.

EXT.–WIDE SHOT INTO CAR FROM OVER SOLDIER'S
SHOULDER–DAY

                    SPENCER
           (handing over everyone's papers)
     You keep good time.

                    AMBERLEA
           (stroking the back of Spencer's neck)
     Must be all that marching.

INT.–GUARD HOUSE
A JUNIOR OFFICER watches through binoculars
as the GUARD at the car reads the documents.
He lowers binoculars and picks up a telephone.

EXT.–WIDE SHOT INTO CAR FROM OVER SOLDIER'S
SHOULDER–DAY

> GLORIA LORRAINE
> (glaring at soldier)
How much longer is this going to take? If I don't get a Dependable soon I'm going to need to use your helmet.

EXT.—WIDE SHOT LOOKING UP TO SOLDIER FROM CAR—DAY
SOLDIER ignores comment and continues to read.

INT.—GUARD HOUSE—WIDE SHOT
A bald SENIOR OFFICER wearing a monocle strides in. JUNIOR OFFICER hands him the binoculars. He looks through them at camera.

EXT.—ZOOM TO CAR LICENSE, FRAMED BY BINOCULAR LENSES—DAY

PAN UP TO TIGHT FOCUS ON BULLET HOLE IN WINDSHIELD

INT.—CLOSE-UP, SENIOR OFFICER'S FACE

SENIOR OFFICER
(lowering binoculars)
Good. Let them through. But follow them. And, Kurt, do it *discreetly.*

ELEVEN

We cross the border at Niagara Falls. I'm not sure if that's where Jer and I came through or not. I didn't pay much attention yesterday on the way down; I was watching *The Three Stooges*. On the way to the border, Gloria Lorraine has AmberLea put the ice in the cooler. She hands her two bottles and a jar. "Gin, vermouth and olives," she says. "I'm going to need a martini later. Now, peel me a banana."

Crossing the border turns out to be easy. Before we get there, she makes Al get back in the trunk. "You and the icing sugar just stay put." Then she has AmberLea drive and tells me to sit in the back.

As we roll up to the crossing, she growls, "My lines. Just look the part." Then she turns into Chatty Granny for the guard. "Well, hellooo. How are you today? Speak up, dear. Yes, hon, I'm Gloria and these are my grandchildren, AmberLea and Spinnaker. We're just driving Spinny back to his home in Toronto. He's been down for a visit. Aren't Fifi and I lucky to have such nice grandchildren to spend time with me?" Fifi is Mister Bones; Gloria Lorraine has him on her lap.

Mister Bones pants, AmberLea's fingers drum the steering wheel, and the lady border guard smiles as if she's going to buy the whole act. No questions about guns, large men with duct-tape burns, bags of white powder, gas tanks, or anything else we might have stashed around the Cadillac. Then she notices the windshield. "Is that a bullet hole?"

"Gracious no." Gloria Lorraine's hands go up to her cheeks, and then she flutters them in front of her. "One of those big trucks just sailed past us and something flew up. I was like to *die*. 'Duck' I yelled. Oh, Miss Fifi didn't like that one bit, did you, Barkums? Poor Spielberg in the back there nearly jumped out of the car."

I almost believe her myself, that's how good she is. The guard, though, looks confused. "Spielberg?" she says.

"Nickname," I say quickly and hold up my camera bag. She laughs and waves us through.

"Good ad lib," says Gloria Lorraine over her shoulder. "From now on, you can call me GL. Now get me to a restroom, pronto."

We stop a few blocks farther on at a Tim Hortons. It's busy, and AmberLea has to pull around the back to find a parking spot, near another Dumpster. It seems to be our day for Dumpsters. Anyway, it's a good spot, because we also have to let Al out of the trunk. He's started thumping again.

"I guess we'd better," says GL, as she eases out of the car. "Too bad. It's a hell of a lot simpler with him in there. Amby, honey, grab those Dependables and help me in there."

"Then can we eat?" AmberLea asks. "I didn't have any breakfast."

It's a good point. Suddenly I realize I'm starving. "Yes, yes," says GL. "Spotty, you let him out, then join us inside." She grabs Mister Bones and her cane and off they go.

I sit for a moment as a couple of cars go by, listening to the thumping; then I pop the trunk and Al boots the lid up. I guess he hurts his foot doing it, because then there's a monologue straight out of *Goodfellas*. I go around and help him out.

"Where's the others?" he grunts, brushing himself off.

"Inside, getting something to eat. And GL has to use the restroom. Let's go in."

Al doesn't answer. Instead, he takes a fistful of my T-shirt and slams me against the side of the Dumpster so hard my glasses fly off. Al has big hands. They make big fists. Black hairs sprout from each of his fingers. He's stronger than he looks, maybe from squishing all that pastry dough. Or maybe from squishing other things. All at once I can believe Al's maybe not just a baker. "Gimme the keys."

He's knocked the breath out of me. I gurgle, "AmberLea has them. She was driving."

"And the old broad has the gun. And Mistah Bones. I can't book it without Mistah Bones."

I nod, fast. The Dumpster is grinding into my back. I register that my head hurts. For no good reason I wonder how strong Jer's hands are. I try to picture him and Al talking pastry dough. It's better than picturing Al tearing me apart and dropping me in the Dumpster.

Al drops my shirt, spins to the car and opens the glove compartment. He curses again. "Why does—?" He turns back to me. "What is it with you kids? Why does nunna yas ever put anything back?"

"W-wha—?" I'm trying to get my breath as I go after my glasses. They've skittered partway under the car.

"There's suppose ta be a shooter and the spare keys in there. I tell my kids, you use somethin', you put it back. Spare keys, spare piece, ya don't just walk off with 'em, for cryin' out loud. What's wrong wit' youse kids today?"

He glares down at me as if it's my fault. With the red streak and partial mustache, he looks a little crazy. People walk by on the way to their cars. Al smoothes out his face. I pull my glasses out and stand up, smoothing out my T-shirt. My hands are shaking. The back of my head still hurts too. "Why don't you just steal a car here and take off?" I say, putting my glasses back on. The frames have gotten bent and now they sit crooked.

Al shakes his head. It looks like he's cooling down. "Not my line. Back inna day, maybe, but now, all the anti-theft computer crap, who can keep up? I can't even hot-wire my own car. But hey, it's a good thing, all the scum out there." He sighs. "Time bein', I'm stuck wit youse. We'll get clean shirts and some-thin' to eat."

It turns out "clean shirts" means new license plates for the Cadillac. Right now it has New York vanity plates that read *CANOLI*. "How do we do that?" I ask.

Al looks at me, then around the Tim's parking lot. "You don't get out much, do ya? What the hell do ya do all day?"

"I watch a lot of movies."

"Like what, *National Geographic* specials?"

From the trunk Al grabs a newspaper and some-thing from a little tool kit. "Okay, you're my straight man. Stand in fronna me." He crouches at the back of the Cadillac. There's an angry little whining noise, then another, a scrape, and then Al is standing beside me, the paper flat under his arm. "C'mawn." I follow him as he strolls to a Matrix parked nearby and bends down as if he has to tie his shoe. Except he's wearing loafers. I step in front of him, hands in pockets, as more people drive by. *Whine, whine, scrape, click, whine, whine.* He's done in seconds.

Al stands up holding his paper, red in the face. Back to the Cadillac. *Click, whine, whine.* We do it again for a front plate. As he finishes, I have a thought. "Why change the plates if it's your car?"

"Let's just say someone's innarested in me," says Al, standing up. "Someone I don't wanna see."

"Why?" I say, trying a little joke. "You miss a delivery?"

Al's head jerks around. He hisses, "Whadda you know about it? I's you, I'd keep my mouth shut. You live longer that way." At this moment Al does not look like your friendly neighborhood birthday-cake baker. Who just happens to carry a gun and keeps another in his car. And gets bound and gagged and stuffed in his own trunk. On bags of white powder. Al looks more like one of those guys from *The Godfather. Mobster* is the word I'm looking for. What have I gotten myself into? I'm rethinking calling Jer, when Al's shoulders slump and his face turns back into a marshmallow.

"C'mawn kid, let's eat while we can."

Inside, there's a lineup. We hit the washroom first. As we whiz, Al says, "So, no offense, but your nonna—your grandma—she got a screw loose or what?"

"She isn't my grandma," I say. "She's AmberLea's grandma. I never met them before today. Her name is Gloria Lorraine and she lives in that retirement home and I just came down to get a kiss from her and film it." Compared to the rest of the day, it sounds almost normal now.

"And film it? What are you, some kinda—?"

"No!" I say. "It's complicated. It's like a last request from my grandpa. She used to be a movie star, his favorite."

"No way!"

"Really." I tell Al some of her movie titles as he zips up.

"So you're honoring your grandpa's dying wish, huh? Straight up?"

I nod.

"Awright, that's A-1. Family, loyalty; that's what it's all about." He nods sharply, then flushes with his elbow. I stand a little straighter as I zip and flush.

When I join Al in the lineup, there's a commotion across the room. I can hear Mister Bones yipping like crazy as GL holds him. He's all wiggles and ears and big eyes, snapping at a guy in a Tim's outfit who's pointing at the *No Pets* notice in the window. AmberLea, chinless, is standing to one side, holding a loaded cardboard takeout tray and staring at a spot on the floor where she's probably wishing a hole would appear that she could disappear into.

TWELVE

"Not a bad cruller," says the King of Cannoli, "but I don't like the coffee."

We're almost back at the car. GL and AmberLea are sitting in the front; Mister Bones is in the back, curled up on what I guess is a Dependable.

"Why are you dragging me along?" AmberLea is saying. "I am so screwed."

"Because I need your help," GL says. "I have to do something important while there's still time."

"Like what, get to a liquor store?"

GL shakes her head. "You're just like me at your age. Won't listen to anyone. And when you won't listen, you do a lot of things you'll regret. Take it from me, you're just getting started. I've had three children and I've been a terrible parent. Your aunt hasn't talked to me in years, your mother runs on Valium, and neither one of them would know happy if it slapped them in the face. I didn't help them; there was no one to help me—well, almost no one—but I can help you. And since you won't listen, I have to show you something."

"I thought I was helping *you*."

"We're helping each other."

"Yeah, right. Great example, Gran. Tell that to my—"

"You'll be back before he even knows you're gone."

"Oh, he'll know all right."

"If there's a problem, I'll deal with it. First, you need to see this. No one knows about this; not your mother, not anyone. You used to like secrets."

"I'm not seven anymore."

"I wish you were. Hush up and eat; we've got a long drive ahead. And it's not as if I'm kidnapping anyone. You came willingly."

"How about me?" says Al, as we come up behind her. He polishes off the cruller, tosses the coffee at a garbage can, reaches into the car and casually grabs GL's scarf at the back of her neck. "Let's cut the crap," he says, still chewing. "Gun, keys, now." With his other hand, he snatches GL's bag from her lap.

I freeze in mid-bite of my bagel and cream cheese.

"Don't be stupid," GL croaks. "Let go of me or AmberLea starts screaming."

"Oh yeah? Sounds to me as if she'd rather call a cab home."

There's a long moment where we're all frozen. People stroll past with coffees. Then AmberLea quavers, "Yeah, let her go or"—she snatches the keys out of the ignition, where we now see they've been all along—"or these are gone."

"Not with Mistah Bones they're not," grunts Al. He's pawing the bag, one-handed, wedging it against the side of the car. "Where's the *gun*?" he hisses.

"Not there," GL gurgles.

AmberLea holds the keys high. Mister Bones jumps up, tail wagging, ready to play. She ignores him. Now she's all chin. "Let her go."

"Here!" I say around a mouthful of bagel and cream cheese. I skip away from Al, behind the trunk. AmberLea tosses me the keys. Al makes a pathetic jump, swats and misses as the bag falls to the pavement.

Mister Bones loves it; he starts jumping too, and yapping like crazy. GL gurgles again. Miraculously, I catch the keys without dropping my bagel. "Pop the trunk," I call to AmberLea. "Show the world what's in there while Al does another Dumpster dive."

Al turns to me, his hand still twisting GL's scarf and gives me a look right out of *Scarface*. "I'll kill her right h—" Suddenly, his face explodes in a grin and he lets go, waving both hands at me. "Awright, awright." He laughs. "You can drive. Family joke!" he says over my shoulder. I look around. Half a dozen people are watching, all holding takeout. I grin at them, too, and pump my fist in the air like an idiot, waving the keys. They all smile or nod in a puzzled kind of way and move on.

Al's good mood disappears. Behind him, GL slumps against the seat, panting. She gasps, "I thought we already dealt with this. Baker, shmaker, you're on the lam. I've been around enough mobsters to know what you are. Right now we're the best cover you can get…And you owe us for getting you and those bags across the border. So choose right now: team up or split up, but no more of this. What's it going to be?"

"Awright." The King of Cannoli—or whatever he really is—sags again. "Let's go."

"Spaceman drives," says GL. "You and AmberLea in the back."

"I should have brought sunscreen," says AmberLea.

"There's some in my bag. And Al, hat and wig on. You're already pink up top."

Al touches the top of his head. "Aw, geez."

I get behind the wheel and start up the car and the GPS, still chewing the last of the bagel.

"Torrance, Ontario," says GL, "Ten fifty Keeler Road. If we can get that far today, we're fine."

As we get back on the highway, AmberLea says from the back, "Gramma, did you say you had *three* kids?"

GL doesn't say anything.

THIRTEEN

Torrance sounds familiar to me. The GPS gets us on the QEW highway and we head toward Toronto. Al slouches in the back, chin on chest. Mister Bones snoozes on his Dependable. AmberLea puts in earbuds and slathers on more sunscreen. In the mirror I watch the wind whip her hair. GL hasn't said a word since Tim Hortons. For a while she watches the landscape. There's not much to see; it's glarey and flat. I wish I had clip-ons for my bent glasses.

After a while I can't tell if she's still watching or if she's snoozing. Then, as we rumble off the Burlington Skyway, she reaches in her jacket pocket and says, without looking at me, "Tell me about your grandfather."

Oh, man. What am I supposed to say? I know it sounds bad, but I haven't thought much about Grandpa since he died, except for this assignment stuff. What pops into my head now is a time when I was maybe seven or eight. Grandpa was sitting on the couch between me and Bunny and we were watching *Bugs Bunny*, and Deb came in and said, "You know how Jer and I feel about the violence in those, Dad," and Grandpa said, "They didn't do you any harm. C'mon, we're having fun here." Bun yelled, "Fun!" and Grandpa snuggled us closer.

That's not going to cut it, so I say, "Well, uh, he was pretty big. Tall, I mean, not like me. He ran a business and he traveled a lot for work, but we always saw him on our birthdays and holidays at the cottage. And he'd come to Bunny's soccer games." And our middle school graduations and school plays, and he babysat us when we were younger. I bet that's where the *Bugs Bunny* thing comes from. I'd forgotten a lot of that stuff.

"Who's Bunny?" GL asks.

"My brother. He's two years younger than me. His real name is Bernard. We just call him Bunny, to not mix him with our other grandpa, Bernie." The wind flattens out our voices and whips them away.

"Uh-huh. But your grandpa—*David,* is that right?—where did he live?"

"Toronto, but like I said, he traveled a lot. He owned his own airplane because he loved to fly. He was a pilot in the war. He'd fly to see my cousin in Buffalo or up to the lake or, well, all over."

"Ahhh," says GL. "Good. I'm glad. Did he take you flying?"

"A couple of times. Bunny loved it, but I didn't. First time, he did this loop thing. Bunny laughed like crazy. I barfed." I don't have to tell her how scared I was and how I started crying. I shouldn't even have said this much.

"What did he say about that?" GL shifts in her seat to look at me.

"Oh, he said he'd seen guys do worse in planes during the war and that one time he'd been so scared he peed himself."

"Well, there you go."

I shrug. "Yeah, but I knew he was mad. I mean, none of my cousins barfed. At least I don't think they did. And Grandpa had war medals and all, so how scared could he have been?"

"Hmph," GL says. "Plenty, would be my guess. Anyway, I don't think he was the one that was mad at you."

I'm not even going to ask what that means.

GL asks, "How many cousins are there?"

"Six," I say. "No, wait, the lawyer said there's one cousin none of us has ever met, but there are six of us who know each other."

GL frowns. "Lawyer?" she says.

"When Grandpa died." I tell her about the will and how we all got our sealed envelopes.

"And you got me," says GL.

"Well, he left me another envelope too. In case you were dead or, like, a vegetable or something."

"How thoughtful. What was plan B?" She gets out a cigarette.

"I don't know. I wasn't supposed to look in the other envelope unless I had to. It's in my camera bag. I was going to read it if you were—"

"I get the picture." She punches the lighter button. "Let's cut to the chase. What did your grandfather say about me?"

I shrug again. "Just that you were his all-time favorite movie star and that you were still alive even though you're older than he was."

"Never talk about a woman's age." She lights up the cigarette. "And that's all he said?" She sounds a little disappointed.

"Well, Mom said that she and her sisters all had to watch your TV shows when they were growing up, and he'd always watch when your movies were on TV. And that he went to see *Drive-In Savages* even though everyone told him not to."

"Very sweet. Not even I saw that stinker. What can I say? I needed the money."

I glance over. Sure enough, GL isn't smoking the cigarette, she's posing with it. Like an old-time movie star. She looks straight ahead and says, "What does your grandmother think of all this?"

"My grandma died when my mom and her sisters were little."

"Well, why didn't—oh, never mind." She waves her cigarette, brushing away whatever she's thinking. "Your mother. What does she do?"

"She teaches philosophy. At York University."

"Very impressive. What about Rip Van Winkle back there?"

"My dad? Um, he writes a column called 'Front Porch Farmer,' for the *Parkdale Advertiser*. It's about—"

"I can guess. What else does he do?"

"Well, he's writing a novel. And refinishing the stairs. And he does a lot of baking."

"Of course. And his father's Grandpa Bernie. Let me guess, Grandpa Bernie was an orgasmic farmer or whatever they're called."

"No, he's a potter on this place called Saltspring Island. It's out west. He had a mime troupe in San Francisco. He was really good. You should see his ladder climbing; he—"

"Spare me." GL holds up a hand. "Your cousins. What do they have to do?"

I tell her about Spain and France and Africa and Bunny's tattoo. Which reminds me, I should text him.

"You must have been thrilled with this assignment," GL says drily. "Why you?"

I can't say, *Because he didn't like me much*, so I say, "I guess because I like movies. I'm going to film school in the fall."

"Film school. Hmph. So's AmberLea, if she ever... Never mind. In my day you only called it *film* if you wore a beret. We called it *pictures* and you *worked* in them. Nobody did *film studies*. Never mind that either. What are you thinking?"

"Huh?"

"For our scene. Profiles? Tight two-shot? How do you want to frame it? You light me from the right and only shoot my left side, clear? And I'm closer to the camera, it's my scene."

"Oh, uh—"

"Cut or fade?"

"Well—"

"And let's be clear right now: no tongues and I don't do nudity."

I almost drive off the road.

"Easy there. Just kidding. Peck on the cheek; your right, my left. How do you set it up? What's your establishing scene?"

"My—?"

"What comes before? You can't just shoot a two-second cheek buss. Who wants to watch that?"

"I don't know, I—"

"I thought you said you wanted to make pictures. I'm giving you the chance of a lifetime here, and you should damn well appreciate it. You're working with a Hollywood star on your first feature. What have you shot so far?"

"Uh…nothing."

"*Nothing?* Why the hell not? Listen, Quentin Maraschino or whatever your name is, what did your Grandpa David tell you to do?"

"Make a movie?"

"I'll do the asking. Of course, make a movie. Of what?"

"Us kiss—I mean, me getting a kiss from you."

"Well, that's not a whole movie. Set up, intro, action, climax, clinch, fade. What's wrong with you? Get shooting."

"Shooting what?"

"*This.* Your grandpa said, *Make a movie.* Look at what I'm giving you here. What more do you want?"

"But this is just…stuff. Real life. It's weird, but there's no story or anything."

Her painted-on eyebrows go up, and I can tell she's probably rolling her eyes behind her sunglasses.

"No sto—You really don't know anything, do you? It's all in the editing. Life is a movie with no jump cuts. It's the cutting that makes the movie."

"But—"

"Skip it." GL sighs. "Just my luck for my last picture; the story of my career." She flicks ash from her cigarette, takes a deep breath. "How did your grandpa die?"

"He just died. In his sleep."

"Good exit." GL nods. "I should be so lucky. I don't have a history of smooth exits." She throws the cigarette away. "And watch your driving. You follow too close. I can't exit yet."

FOURTEEN

After that, GL clams up and pretty soon she's snoozing. That's fine with me, even though she snores. I'm still pretty steamed by that "you don't know anything" crack. I mean, what has there been worth filming? GL shooting the gun maybe, with Al tied up? Yeah, right. I can imagine how happy Al would be, all over YouTube. I'm still a little sore from the last time he grabbed me.

The traffic gets really busy and I have to concentrate. It's too weird for anyone to believe anyway. Life is not a movie. A movie is heroes and hot girls and special effects and adventures and excitement, not real life. AmberLea is not Hollywood hot. Driving old ladies up to cottage country to get a kiss on the cheek is not *Fast and Furious*. Al—well, I've got to admit I still don't get how Al fits in. If he's for real, then he's the one thing that could be from a movie.

And then I get it: what we're doing. What we're doing is *Gloria Lorraine trying to make her life into a movie*. Of course. She just said, *My last picture* and *Look what I'm giving you here*. This is her little fantasy, and she's dragging me and AmberLea along for the ride. I bet Al is a washed-up actor too. Probably even his mustache was fake. I bet she's hired him to act this out.

And then I *really* get it, and it's even worse than I thought. What if Grandpa worked this out with Gloria Lorraine, to give me a fake adventure, one that I could handle, instead of a real adventure, like climbing Mount Kilimanjaro. I guess a tattoo and a road trip are all he figured Bun and I would be up for. I'm surprised he didn't just have Bunny order a T-shirt. Oh, man. And to think I really got into it there, blowing off Jer and acting like a character in a B movie at the border and in the Tim's parking lot.

Now I'm totally bummed. I drive up Highway 427 and then crawl along the 401 to Highway 400, where we go north again. All the time I'm wishing I could just pull over and walk away. That would be tricky on a major freeway. Besides, even though Toronto is my town, I don't exactly know where I am. Then I do start to recognize stuff, because this is the way to Grandpa's cottage too. By now it's about two thirty in the afternoon, so it's getting crazy busy here too, on a summery Friday. It would take me forever to get home from here. I keep driving.

Before we get to Barrie, I pull into a highway service center. We gas up, then park. I take Mister Bones over to the rest area, which is a patch of grass with some picnic tables under a few trees. The others go inside. I don't really want to deal with them right now.

Mister Bones does his thing, and I check for messages while I think over what to do. There are two from Bunny. The last one reads, did u look yet? tel me. I flip back through his messages, and there it is: a photo of his tattoo. It's a weird one. Instead of a mosquito with a cigar and a machine gun, there's a striped number fifteen and, beside it, a birthday candle that I guess is supposed to be blown out. What the…? Maybe Bun chose it instead because he's fifteen. Who knows? Right now I'm so bummed I don't really care. I text back, very cool what will u get when u r 16? I skip the messages from Deb and Jer and shut off the phone. Having my whole pretend "adventure" stage-managed by Grandpa is bad enough; I don't need parents looking over my shoulder too.

I stare at Highway 400 and wonder if I should just try hitchhiking home. Maybe that would be an adventure. Then I get a better idea: if GL wants a movie, she can have one. Only this one is going to show the whole thing for the load of bull it really is.

I lug Mister Bones back to the car and get my new video camera from the trunk, where it's nestled between the icing sugar—or whatever—and the gas cylinder. Mister Bones and I head back to the shade. When I take the camera out of its case, Grandpa's second envelope falls out. I stuff it back in. It hardly matters now. Anyway, it's probably a ticket to a Disney movie and money for an ice-cream cone.

At least the camera is very cool. It has HD and an extra powerful zoom. I take off the lens cap and hit the Power button. The battery is charged up; I'd done that to get ready for this morning. On the view screen, I see the toes of my Converse One Stars. I raise the camera, bend over the screen and do a slow sweep around the parking lot. Cars pulling in and out, people stretching, taking little kids by the hand, a couple of other people with dogs.

I keep going until I get the Caddy in the shot, way across the baking asphalt. Then the whole scene is blanked out as a black Lincoln Navigator with tinted windows rolls past my lens. So I track it all the way to the far bay of the gas bar. I try the zoom, just a little. The driver gets out and goes to the pump. He's superskinny, in a preppy navy blazer, khakis and a pink shirt. He looks like Adrien Brody with boat shoes. Then a guy who looks like King Kong in a polo shirt gets out of the passenger side and helps a little old man out of the backseat. I zoom in more. The old dude is wearing a red blazer and a yellow shirt with a green tie and a snappy white straw hat. His shoes match his hat. Down by my ankles, Mister Bones begins to growl.

FIFTEEN

As King Kong and the old man shuffle in one door of the service center, I pull back and pick up AmberLea, GL and a bulky guy coming out another. The guy's in a Toronto Maple Leafs cap and a green T-shirt with white blobs that spell *Ontario Rocks*. Mister Bones stops growling. I zoom in tight this time. Ontario Rocks is Al. What was left of the mustache is gone. Mister Bones perks up right away and starts yipping. Al's head swivels, and they come over to us.

"Whattaya filming?" Al asks suspiciously.

"Is my hair right?" says GL. "Never shoot without setup, Stanley."

"Just getting some *real life*." I make it sound as sarcastic as possible.

"Lemme see." Al peers at the screen. GL crowds in with him. I play it back. Al's eyes widen as the black Lincoln comes into focus. As the old man gets helped out of the car, Al blurts out some foreign words that I'm pretty sure are obscene.

GL says, "Well, what a coincidence. There's Rocco Wings. You'd think the old devil was following me."

It hits me that it's the old guy from Erie Estates, only without the big glasses. Did she arrange this too? Wow, it's getting complicated.

"He's not following you." Al is practically hyperventilating as he looks over to the SUV. "He's following *me*. Those are the guys who wanna ice me." I have to hand it to him: he's a good actor; a little over the top maybe, but good.

"Rocco?" says Gloria Lorraine. "So you *are* mobbed up. I knew it. Why didn't you say so? I'll talk to him. He eats out of my hand. He's seen *Blond Trust* eleven times." She turns toward the service center.

"No!" Al grabs her arm. "You can't. It's complicated. See, I was supposed to, uh, pick up something for him—for them—just as a favor, you unnerstand."

"I'll bet you were," says GL. "Something that looks a lot like icing sugar?"

"Well, yeah. But the delivery guy never showed up. Only they don't believe me."

"I'm not surprised, given what's in your trunk."

"Aw, for the luvva—" Al smacks his own forehead. "I told them, I told you, I keep *tellin'* everybody, that's not—Aw, never mind. Point is, they think I tried to double-cross them, steal their merchandise, so they wanna ice me. Those two guys are Rocco's sons, Vince and Tiffy; they snatched me and Mistah Bones this morning. Said the old guy wanted to do me personal. He's extra mad because they need the classic right now. Word is, they're doing some kind of three-way deal, with some fancy-named gang—not even a "gang," a whaddyacallit—and a bunch of bikers, all outta state…guns, drugs, cash, the usual. I don't know more than that and you don't wanna. They kept me out of the loop."

Classic? I wonder. Maybe Al's right; I don't get out enough. Before I can ask what "classic" is, GL cuts in, waving a hand.

"Rocco shakes so much he couldn't put a bullet in a barn. He'll be in a better mood after he uses the restroom. Prostate problems. Look, he's coming out now."

Sure enough, the old guy is shuffling back out with King Kong Wings. "Get down!" Al hisses. He crouches behind me at the picnic table.

I sigh. For a second there I was into it, but there's a little problem with this scene. Casually I say, "So, how did they know to come here?"

"Who knows?" Al moans, from somewhere behind my knees. "How did they know where I was this morning when I went for the pickup?"

AmberLea lifts her shades to the top of her head and looks at me, dead-on, for the first time. "A GPS transmitter," she says. "Like in—"

"*Red Means Go*," I finish for her. "Matt Damon, Angelina Jolie, Jeff Bridges, 2008." I can't help it, it's a movie. "And they tracked the guy by a GPS attached to—"

"The dog," she finishes for me. AmberLea scoops up Mister Bones and grabs at his collar. He struggles and yips. I reach over and feel along the leather. There's a bump under the metal buckle. I reach under and twist at it and off pops a button-sized something. What the…?

"I bet it's a magnetized transmitter," says AmberLea.

"Ditch it," Al babbles. "Whatever it is, ditch it, *fast*."

"I'll do it," says AmberLea. "Nobody's seen me."

She takes the thing from me, puts Mister Bones down and starts across the parking lot toward an Ontario Provincial Police cruiser. Meanwhile, Adrian Brody Wings has finished gassing up. He's moved the suv closer to the service center doors. He and King Kong Wings are putting Rocco Wings back inside the Lincoln again.

"Maybe they'll just go." Al is peeking over the picnic table. "If they get ahead of us, we're golden."

"They won't go as long as the GPS tells them they should be here," I say. Then I remind myself not to believe this junk. For a second there, I was into it again. It's hard not to get sucked in.

Sure enough, KK Wings scans the parking lot. Now AB Wings heads for the service center. In his navy blazer he scuttles through knots of tourists in bright summer clothes like a cockroach in a candy store.

I look the other way. AmberLea is at the OPP cruiser, one hand resting on the roof as she bends down to the driver's window. I rethink my position on her butt being too big for skinny jeans.

"No cops!" Al hisses.

"Hush," says GL. "Trust me. Police are not her favorite either. Do you really own a bakery too?"

"Yes, I own a bakery!" Al sounds genuinely hurt. "I'm the King of Cannoli."

"So you're just a gangster on the side."

"Hey, let's just say I'm diversified. I got innaresting friends."

"Or family."

"Call them cousins."

AmberLea starts back toward us as AB Wings comes out of the service center. Behind her, the cruiser starts up. Now AB is looking around. He begins walking a slow sweep of the parking lot. For now his view of the Caddy is blocked by a Chevy van with cheesy-looking wolves painted on the side. He turns the other way. As he does, he reaches beneath that blue blazer and gives a little tug at the small of his back. Anyone who's ever seen an action movie has to think, Gun. Oh, please. I roll my eyes.

"At the very least," Al croaks, "lemme have the piece and you get outta here before someone gets hurt."

"I can't," GL says, lighting a smoke and posing at the picnic table. "I left it in the toilet tank of that donut shop at the border."

Al groans and mutters more foreign-language swear words. I turn on my camera. What else is there to do?

"That's more like it. Remember, left side only," Gloria Lorraine murmurs, looking away and not moving her lips. "And keep the damn light behind you."

AmberLea joins us as the cruiser rolls past. "Easy," she says. "I asked how long to Torrance 'cause I got texted there was an accident up the highway. She's going to check it out. I left the transmitter up by her light rack. Now the suv will follow it."

"Right. Unless they spot the Caddy first." I must sound too sarcastic. She looks at me and does the disappearing-chin thing. I'm tempted to make sure they spot the car. Then they can act this out and maybe I'll be home by suppertime.

Sure enough, AB Wings turns back toward the Caddy. As he does, two things happen at once: the wolf van backs out, blocking his view; and there's a shout from KK Wings at the suv. AB looks back. KK is waving frantically. Beyond him, you can just see the OPP cruiser accelerating onto the highway. AB Wings starts to run. When he hops in the suv, it barrels away too. How the heck did they do that? I wonder. Is this—? It can't be for real. Can it?

Behind me, Al blows out a big shaky breath and stands up. "Good move widda GP thing. I owe ya."

"You already owe us for this morning," says Gloria Lorraine, stubbing out her cigarette on the picnic table. "Now let's get going. AmberLea, honey, primo move. Help me up. And no filming while I walk. My fans don't need to see me totter."

I follow them back, still puzzling it all out. We get back to the car and something else hits me: that's a real bullet hole in the windshield. I totter a little myself. Now I don't know what to think.

SIXTEEN

AmberLea drives. We take Highway 11 north of Barrie. I sit in the back with Al all the way to Gravenhurst. Al smokes a cigar. I try to figure out what's going on: real or fake? Did Grandpa plan this? And if he didn't plan it, did he know something weird might happen? But how could...? And if they...? In the end, it's too complicated. All I can come up with is, Go with it. Maybe it is a movie. In the movies they always go for the ride. And as soon as I think that, I feel lighter. I'll take the ride.

On the way to Gravenhurst we don't see any black Lincolns, but everyone notices how the land gets rockier. "We're getting up north now," I call over the wind.

"North?" GL laughs. "Don't kid yourself. This is barely even south."

Americans think they know everything.

We hit town around four thirty. GL calls for a grocery stop. "Dinner and breakfast," she orders, pulling out American bills.

"You prob'ly couldn't cook your way outta a paper bag," Al says. "The kid and I will deal widdit. Where we goin'? Full kitchen?"

"Play it safe," says GL. "Think barbecue."

When Al and I come out of the store, GL is yapping into a cell phone, AmberLea has her chin tucked in again and Mister Bones is just yapping. "Well, I need her," GL snaps. "Really? I raised *you* didn't—all right, Consuela raised you. Be glad I paid her; she earned every penny…It's nobody's damn business…Monday…they won't even know she's been gone…How? They're not the damned FBI, they're just a two-bit…Oh for god's sake, house arrest is *nothing*. Little Moe used to… Listen, I'll talk to them. She can call it community service. She has to do that too, doesn't she?

We'll be in touch." She shoves the phone at AmberLea, who shuts it down.

Al's ears have pricked up at *FBI* and *house arrest*. Mine too, actually. There's a kind of embarrassed quiet as we stash the groceries in the trunk. Then GL says, "Let's go." She looks tired. "I need a martini. And a Dependable."

We take Highway 169 out of town. Torrance turns out to be a bundle of houses about fifteen minutes away. The GPS takes us past a church and a little community center. Then we turn and cross some railway tracks and chug along a gravel lane away from the houses. We cross a little channel and suddenly see a lake and cottages, and then we're in trees. The number marker for 1050 is blue with white numerals, like at Grandpa's. We turn down a dirt track. The trees have homemade wooden signs with family names on them. Beyond you can see cabins and cottages and a couple of places as big as AmberLea's house. "Look for Karpuski," GL orders.

"Karpuski?"

"An alias. For privacy. Didn't want fans nosing around back when I bought this. And put the top up as soon as we stop. The bugs will be bad."

We pull in at the sign. There's another one on the tree below it. It's got the name of a real estate company on it and it says *SOLD*. There's a parking spot in the trees, beside someone's golf cart. "Bought this in '53," GL says. "Not even your mother knows about it, Amby. Haven't been here in years. I pay a local to look after it and rent it out. I told him I was coming up for a last visit. It should be ready for us."

The first mosquitoes have started their bombing runs as the top goes up. AmberLea helps her grandma out of the car. Al and I grab the groceries.

We stumble along a path, past a woodpile and a rickety-looking outhouse painted white and green. The wooden cabin is painted brown, and the wood has been rounded to look like logs. There's a key behind the electric meter. We crowd into the little back kitchen, one step ahead of the bugs.

"Old-timey," Al puffs. And it is; not fancy either. I slide past him. The front room is all wood, with big saggy chairs and a couch and a huge stone fireplace. Out front is a screened porch with a hammock and a picnic table. Outside I can see a giant rock perched on a slope that goes down to the dock and lake.

It's so familiar it's weird. "This is exactly like my Grandpa's cottage," I say. "He said a cottage was for showing up, not for showing off."

"Exactly," GL says behind me. "They built this place from a kit you could buy, back in the thirties. There were a lot of them. Where is your grandpa's?"

"Port Carling," I say. That much I know. "Bala is near here, right? We go there sometimes."

"I'll be damned." GL shakes her head. "All those years, all he had to do was look in the phone book."

"Wouldn't it say *Karpuski*?"

"Well, so—Oh, yes. I see what you mean," she says and turns away. She's headed for what I see is a bathroom at the back of the cottage. I'm glad we don't have to use the outhouse.

Al pops out of the kitchen. "Okay, the groceries are put away. Now there's gotta be swimsuits here somewheres. C'mon, kid." Suddenly he's Susie Homemaker. I go along anyway. All at once I feel how dusty and sticky I am. Sure enough, there are a couple of suits hanging in the back bedroom. I pull one on. I'd never do this at Grandpa's. This is different, somehow. The suit is pretty big, but I don't care— until I remember AmberLea. I wrap a towel around me and hustle out. Schwarzenegger I'm not. The dock is in sunlight, so the bugs aren't bad. Al is already in the water, just his head and hairy shoulders sticking out. "Jump in," he says. "Water's good."

SEVENTEEN

I take off my glasses and shoes and jump in. The water rips away everything I've been feeling. I'd forgotten it's only June. I come up gasping and paddling.

"Geez," says Al, "I didn't say right on toppa me."

As I get used to the water, I look up at the cottage. Except for the brown paint it is a lot like Grandpa's—only I'd never jump in the lake there. No, I'd be where a slightly blurry AmberLea is right now, watching us from the screened-in porch. "C'mon in," I call up to her.

She shakes her head. "Can't," she says. "No suit." I think over the possibilities of AmberLea swimming without a suit. Is this going to be that kind of movie? I wish.

I paddle some more. Al floats on his back. He's got more insulation than me. Except for the top of his head, he is the hairiest guy I've ever seen. "First time I've relaxed all day," he sighs. "I'm gettin' too old for this."

It's hard for me to talk back. In fact, it's hard for me to even think back. Is that something a real mobster would say? Or an actor pretending to be one? It sounds a lot like *Sopranos*. Go with it or drown, I think. I'm not such a hot swimmer. Bunny is totally into water-skiing and windsurfing and all that stuff, like our cousins, but I'm not. Those things have always scared me a little, to tell the truth, and after Jer and I tipped the canoe when I was ten, I didn't want to do that either.

In fact, to *really* tell the truth, when I was younger I wouldn't even have sat where AmberLea is now. I used to have what I thought was a secret place under the porch, where I'd go to read comics and stuff. Grandpa didn't allow electronics at the cottage, not even TV. One summer under there, I told Bun every story I could remember from this cool old TV series I'd found on video, called *The Twilight Zone*.

And I remember being under there another time when my cousins were all playing tag, but I was watching Grandpa and Bunny down on the dock, not far away. It was really strange. Bunny was saying he was sorry to Grandpa. And when Grandpa said he shouldn't feel sorry, Bunny said he wasn't sorry for himself, he was sorry for Grandpa. Then DJ, I think, came running down to the dock and pushed Bunny in the water. Then Grandpa pushed DJ in. And then somebody pushed Grandpa in. Nobody pushed me in. I watched the whole thing and nobody found me.

But now I'm in.

Dinner is good. Al has made burgers and Caesar salad. "Real dressing, not bottle crapola." Like Jer, he's big on garlic. Right now, he's saying to GL, "So, you really were in movies?" GL has made them both martinis in juice glasses. She's got a second little plate beside her glass with all her pills on it.

I want to say, "So, house arrest: good times?" to AmberLea, but I'm guessing this isn't such a great icebreaker.

She says, "Your grandpa had a place like this, huh?"

"Yeah," I say. "We'd go up and water-ski and windsurf and stuff." Okay, okay—you'd have said the same thing. Anyway, this is the time at the cottage I almost loved, when everyone was having dinner and talking all at once and I could just listen and not have to say anything, except maybe when I had to help Bun a little. And I'm not sure what counts more, the "almost" or the "loved." See, there's a worm in the apple, like there always was with me and Grandpa.

I find myself telling AmberLea, "At Grandpa's there were two picnic tables end to end, to make one big long table so we could all sit together. Grandpa would sit at the end, in a chair, to make room, and he had this trick he liked to play. The plastic table cloth hung over the sides of the table, and when people weren't watching he'd curl up his end of the plastic under the table—like an eaves trough—and he'd pour water into it. If you were paying atten-tion, you'd see the water coming and lift up the plastic too, so the water would run past you. If you weren't, it would run into your lap. And then you'd jump up and everyone would laugh."

Grandpa got Jer a lot, 'cause Jer would always get all involved in the conversation. Jer would always laugh when he got wet. I almost cried the time it happened to me. After that, I was always worried that I wasn't paying enough attention. I'd watch extra hard, and I'd laugh extra hard when he got someone else, just out of relief. And now I don't even know why I'm telling AmberLea about it.

"Eww," says AmberLea. "That's mean."

I think, She's right. Weird thing is, though, it makes me feel a little bad for Grandpa. Not exactly sure why.

Meanwhile, GL is saying something about doing live TV with Paul Newman, and Al is eating it up faster than his burger. She stops to scoop up a handful of pills and swallow them with the last of her martini. She looks out over the lake. "Haven't seen anything like this in a long time."

After dinner, Al goes out to put the tarp from the woodpile over the car. Even though we've ditched the Wings, and have "clean shirts," he says he's still nervous about being spotted. *Go with it.* GL, car keys in pocket, sits on the porch in the evening sun. AmberLea and I get to clean up. I wash.

She doesn't say anything for a long time. Finally I ask if she's seen her grandma's movies.

"Some," she says, drying a glass. "They're pretty boring, except for a couple of the mystery ones. And they're hard to find. I mean, we're not talking *Star Spawn* here."

"Thank god," I say, scrubbing. "I hated that."

"Oh, totally." She nods and takes a plate out of the rack. "Have you seen *Stress Fracture* yet?"

"No, it's on my *Got To* list. I downloaded the three trailers, but it hasn't opened yet."

"It has in New York. I went, before my—Anyway, it was awesome. There was this divided-screen bit where you follow all four of them and they're all getting to where the bomb is, only they don't know each other yet so they're in each other's shots from different angles and—"

"Like in *Crossfire*—"

"Yeah, just like that, and—"

We talk movies and TV shows until the dishes are done. It's fun. Then I almost blow it. We're been talking about *Arrested Development,* and without thinking I blurt out, "Hey, are you really under house arrest?"

AmberLea instantly turns as pink as Al's sunburned head and her chin vanishes again. She gives this teeny nod. "It was stupid," she says, her chin still gone. "A bunch of us were partying and we called a cab to take us home and we gave this address near all our places, and when we got there we all jumped out and ran instead of paying. It was a plan, like, but we'd been, um…you know, so we weren't thinking too straight and the cab driver just called the cops and followed us. We didn't even think to split up. We had to go to court and everything. We all got fines and house arrest for a month, except for writing our finals. For a while the judge wasn't even going to let us do that; I would've lost my whole senior year. Anyway, the judge, she said if we liked getting around so much, we could try staying put for a while. So now I'm not even supposed to be outside, let alone here, and I have to wear—Oh, never mind. It was my own fault. I was really dumb. Anyway, 'scuse me." She puts the dishtowel down and brushes past me into the front room.

I follow her, praying I haven't completely blown it. I want to make her feel better, but I don't have a clue what to say. Maybe I could tell her something dorky I've done. On the other hand, the stuff I've done is so *completely* dorky it would probably make me seem stupid instead of sympathetic.

When I get to the front room, Al is plunked down in a chair, texting and muttering to himself about no signal. He's trying to message his agent, a flour company, or the Godfather, I guess, depending on what's real. It *is* hard to tell. I mean, how many gangsters have I met? I don't have a lot to go on here. For that matter, how many bakers have I met, apart from Jer and his Boys Bake club? I'm guessing there aren't any Goodfellas hiding in there, or the philosophy department at York U either, but I could be wrong.

I look past Al. GL is still on the porch, in the last of the evening sun. AmberLea has picked up the remote for a TV in the corner. "They probably only get one channel," I say. I figure it's better than saying nothing.

"No," she says. "Didn't you see the satellite dish on the roof?"

The screen blips on. She surfs maybe ten or fifteen channels before she stops and clicks back to one. There, in glorious black and white, a blond is pointing a pistol at a man behind a desk. A familiar voice purrs, "You know, shooting a man is like straightening your stockings. A lady's not supposed to do it, but sometimes you have to."

"Aw, c'mon baby," the man says, and then I don't hear the rest because I'm thinking what Al says out loud. "*It's her.*" Al has put down his cell. AmberLea and I are both leaning forward. And it is her; it's the Gloria Lorraine I saw on the Wikipedia site. And she's a very sexy babe in an old-fashioned kind of way, walking around the desk with a gun in her hand.

"I seen this," Al breathes.

"*Shadow Street*," says AmberLea.

"That's Fred MacMurdo," says Al as the man stands, pushes the gun away and locks Gloria Lorraine in a hot kiss.

"He had awful breath," says a voice beside us. We look up to see the real thing. "He'd have bourbon for breakfast and liver and onions for lunch," GL goes on, leaning on her cane, "and he just reeked. We must have shot that scene ten times too, because he kept blowing his tag line. I was like to throw up at the end. Probably did it out of spite because they gave the good angle to me."

Onscreen, Fred MacMurdo in a hat looks out a windshield as he drives through the rain. "God, what a weasel he was," says GL, "and a bum-grabber to boot. Barbara Stanwyck said the same thing. Amby, turn that off. We have things to discuss."

EIGHTEEN

AmberLea hits the Mute button. GL says, "Now, come out here." She's got a map spread on the picnic table. "Here's where we're going." She puts on a big pair of glasses. Her flame-red fingernail stabs at the map. We all squeeze in to look. She's pointing to the north shore of Lake Superior.

"Terrace Bay?" AmberLea squints.

"Or Marathon. We can be there by Sunday night if we get as far as Sault Sainte Marie tomorrow. Then we can go to Jackfish Monday morning."

"What's Jackfish?" says Al.

"Too small to be on the map," says GL, "but it's right here." She taps a little pocket of the lake where it dents in before Terrace Bay. "I have to do something there. Before I'm done, if you know what I mean."

"Like what?" AmberLea's chin goes away again.

"I'll explain when we get there. A lady's not a woman without a secret."

"That's from a movie too," Al says.

"*Blond Trust*," says Gloria Lorraine. "It was an ad-lib muff. The line was supposed to be 'A lady's not a lady without a secret.' Normie Bly, the director, liked it so much he kept it."

"Yeah, yeah," says Al. "*Blond Trust*. That was you? With what's-his-name, skinny guy, where he pushes—"

"—the old man in the wheelchair down the elevator shaft," she finishes for him, "and giggles."

"I loved that," says Al. "You were great. They use ta play it on the late movie on Channel 7 alla time when I was a kid. Grew up with a guy, Mikey, just like that. 'Mikey,' we'd say, 'You're on!'" Al shakes his head. "The stuff he'd get up to."

"Where is he now?" I ask.

Al shrugs. "Last I saw, he was hanging off a balcony and the guy holding him remembered he had to go make a call."

"Oh," I say. "That's, uh, too bad."

"Depends on your point of view."

"The point is," GL brings us back, "you get me to Jackfish and you're done. Spicer here gets his kiss and his movie, and, Al, you can take off. If you keep going west you can nip over the border into Minnesota. That would give you some breathing room. And AmberLea can run the camera and learn a thing or two from her gramma before it's too late."

I'm looking at the map while she says it. "Hey," I say, "how come we didn't just keep going up Highway four hundred? It's shorter."

"Because I need something from here before the new owners move in," says GL. "From behind the deer head."

The stuffed deer head is on the living-room wall above the couch. Al is the tallest. And the heaviest. The couch groans and sags as he stands on it. He reaches up. "Behind the base," orders GL. Al fumbles around and comes up with something that he passes down into GL's impatient hand. It's a tarnished locket on a fine chain. GL totters to a chair, jams her glasses back on and struggles with the thing. She gets it open, looks at it for a minute, then snaps it shut. "Get me my purse." AmberLea brings it. GL shoves in the locket, snaps the purse shut, then waves for AmberLea to help her stand up. "I'm off to bed," she says. "I get the front bedroom. Amberlea, you get the middle and you boys take the back. And you two"—she swings a finger from me to AmberLea—"no hanky-panky, got it? I'm up in the night and I'll know."

AmberLea turns into a tomato. I look away; I can feel my own face burning.

"Early start tomorrow." GL turns away. "Don't burn the midnight oil." Leaning on her cane, she shuffles into the bedroom and closes the door.

NINETEEN

It's not even dark out, almost nine o'clock. I decide to try calling Bunny, and then before the light goes, I'll film a little to show my family how much the place is like Grandpa's. Besides, it will keep AmberLea and me from having to look at each other.

I hurry up the shadowy path. Al has done a good job of covering up the car. I curse him as bugs dive-bomb me. I struggle with the tarp and get the camera bag out. Then I hustle down to the dock, where the last rays of the sun still linger. A breeze has sprung up, keeping the mosquitoes away here—which reminds me of Bunny's tattoo. Across the lake a freight train rumbles over a trestle. I put down the camera bag and dig out my phone. The signal out here is good. I debate telling Al, then decide not to. It's nice to be alone for a minute. Bunny answers on the third ring.

"Spencer?"

"Bun-man! How's it going?"

"I'm not going anywhere right now."

"No, I mean what are you doing?"

"Right now we're loading up, me and Jaden and the posse. Did you see my tattoo?"

I figure he must be playing a video game. Bun gets right into them. "Sure did. Ultracool, Bun. What did Deb say about it?"

"She's not here, but Jaden says it's perfect."

Jaden must be a character in the video game. "Well, Deb'll probably be home soon. I'm glad Jaden likes it. But how come a fifteen, Bun?"

"That's what the guy said I needed to be part of the posse."

"What posse?"

"Fifteenth Street Posse. I'm in."

Right. Of course. So Bunny has either gotten a tattoo to go with a video game or he's joined a street gang. I wonder which would bug Deb more. Not that it's my problem; anyway, Bun is better at handling things than most people think. He's probably doing better than me right now. As if he knows what I'm thinking, he says, "Did you kiss your old lady yet?"

"Not yet. Things are a little strange here, Bun. We're up in a place called Torrance."

"Torrance? Where's Torrance? Is that Buffalo?"

"No, Torrance, Ontario."

"Torrance, Ontario?"

"Yeah, it's up near the cottage somewhere."

"Near the cottage? Did Dad let you drive?"

"Well, he's not here."

"Neither is Mom."

"Yeah, I know. Anyway, I'm with the old lady and her granddaughter and this guy named Al Capoli, and I'm driving his white Cadillac convertible."

I wait while Bun repeats all that. It's a habit he has. Then I say, "Okay. Glad everything's cool."

"Oh yeahhh. I'm really pumped."

"Excellent. Gotta run, Bun."

"Aren't you driving?"

"Yeah, I am, I forgot. Later."

I couldn't tell him it might all be a fake. At least he got a for-real tattoo he liked. Unless it's henna.

Would Bunny know the difference? Hey, is it a virtual Fifteenth Street Posse or a real street gang? Drop it, I think. Just go with it.

Before I put the phone away, I peek at how many texts there are from Jer and Deb. Answer: a lot; most from Deb. I think about just deleting them, but then I pick one at random, to see how much they're freaking out.

I check one of Deb's: if u have time or need in NYC call Sylvia at CCNY. u remember her happy to help. Can give you number xoM

What? I scroll to the one before: NYC wow great! glad GL is nice be sure offer to pay expenses with grandpa's money xoM. The one after is Sylvia's phone number and a hotel suggestion.

What has Jer been telling her? I check his latest text. All it says is, If that's all you have to say, I will. Huh? I don't know what that means. What was the last thing I said to him? Right now, I can't remember. I send him a text: all good going north done Monday.

I pocket my phone. That's all I can process for now.

I pick up the camera bag. I figure I can get a good shot of the cottage from here, with the light behind me. When I open the bag, the first thing I see is Grandpa's other envelope. What the heck, I figure, it doesn't matter now. I open it.

Spence,

If Gloria Lorraine is out of the picture, here's your alternate target. Back in the '30s I swung a pick on a road crew, helping build the North Shore highway. Now it's Highway 17, part of the Trans-Canada. I was just a kid, my first time away from home and my first real job. Worst job I ever had too, but in those Depression days I was damn lucky to have it. Lord, the blackflies and deer-flies and mosquitoes! Then one day something else buzzed us: a bush pilot in a Fox Moth. Then and there I decided I had to fly. I know you've heard all this before, a million times, usually as water rolled down the cottage tablecloth. Maybe I shouldn't have done that; maybe I should have just told you the story. Water under the bridge. This is my dishtowel to mop it up with.

Anyway, since Gloria Lorraine and I will both be ghosts—if anything—go to a place I hear is now a ghost town just off that highway and film it for me. The place is called Jackfish. It's not on maps anymore, but you'll find it. Just west of there, the road goes over a rise and around a bend. You'll know it. I was just below that rise when that plane came roaring over it and changed my life. Film it for me as the sun rises behind you. Then film whatever is left of the town, before it's gone too, especially the railroad station and the Superior Hotel. Those places meant a lot to me. What happened there isn't as important as the story you'll make up about it.

Love,

Grandpa

I put the letter in my pocket; then I film. I go up to the cottage. Al passes me in his swimsuit. "One last dip. Comin'?"

I shake my head. Inside, you can hear Gloria Lorraine snoring. In the living room, AmberLea is sitting watching the silent TV. I sit beside her, but not too close. Onscreen, a young Gloria Lorraine holds a cigarette the same way the old one does. She has that knowing look from her head shot. Then it melts to fear. "No," you can see her saying, "No." Then it's Fred MacMurdo looking tough, and he's holding the gun this time. AmberLea, on the other hand, is holding her grandmother's purse. The purse is open in her lap and so is the locket. I lean closer.

Inside the locket is an old yellow-brown photo of a kid—no, a baby.

AmberLea looks at me. "What is going on?"

I wish I knew.

REEL THREE

EXT.—NORTHERN ONTARIO ROAD MEDIUM SHOT,
FROM ROADSIDE—DAY

A white Cadillac, top down, zooms through the frame, left to right, against a background of Northern Ontario rock face. GL's scarf flutters in the breeze.

TRAVELING SHOT, FROM ABOVE—FRONT OF CADILLAC
AND ROAD BEHIND

SPENCER driving, shades on, GL holding hat on head, in back AL (James? you know, from *Sopranos*) smoking cigar, and AMBERLEA. Between them, a food cooler.

LOW RUMBLING NOISE

Camera holds steady as three motorcycles appear around a bend in the road behind them. SPENCER tilts head to check his mirror.

A HIGHER HUMMING NOISE (AS SPENCER TILTS HIS HEAD)

A helicopter closes in above the bikes.

> SPENCER
>> (hitting the gas)
>
> Trouble.

> GL
>> (taking .357 Magnum from glove
>> compartment as car accelerates)
>
> Finally. I was getting bored.

Behind, the helicopter rises.

AERIAL SHOT, FROM BESIDE HELICOPTER AS IT TRACKS THE CADILLAC BELOW

Machine-gun fire shoots from the helicopter. Bullets strike the road beside and in front as the Cadillac swerves from lane to lane.

TRACKING SHOT, FROM ABOVE—FRONT OF CADILLAC
AND ROAD BEHIND (AS ABOVE)

Helicopter is flying low behind car. SPENCER pulls Glock pistol from underneath his jacket and passes it back to AMBERLEA.

SPENCER

Not yet. Shorten the range—and hold on.

SPENCER yanks on steering wheel.

TRACKING SHOT, FROM BEHIND HARLEYS—HARLEYS,
CADILLAC, HELICOPTER

Three Harleys, one with a sidecar, are following the Cadillac. Helicopter just visible ahead and above as it peels away. The bikes are catching up to the Cadillac fast. The road winds, with lots of dips and curves.

MEDIUM WIDE SHOT FROM SIDE OF ROAD—HARLEYS
DRIVING BY

The three Harleys drive by. MAN IN SIDECAR readies a rocket launcher. DRIVER OF LEAD BIKE has machine gun mounted between handlebars.

GRENADE BIKER has grenades on a strap across his chest. DRIVER OF LEAD BIKE fires off a burst as Cadillac swerves.

TRACKING SHOT, FROM ABOVE–FRONT OF CADILLAC AND ROAD BEHIND (AS BEFORE)
AMBERLEA is in firing position over back of car, trying to steady her arm on seat back, trunk.

> AMBERLEA
>
> Don't swerve so much. I can't line up a shot!

BURST OF MACHINE–GUN FIRE
Bullets hit rock face just above car. Dust flies.

WHINE OF RICOCHETS

> AMBERLEA
>
> Swerve! Swerve!

MEDIUM WIDE SHOT, LOOKING FORWARD THROUGH WINDSHIELD OF CADILLAC
Cadillac is driving down the road. Suddenly the helicopter swoops in from in front of Cadillac.

Bullets dot middle of the highway. Cadillac swerves. Bullet knocks driver's side mirror off and then helicopter is past.

SHOT FROM BEHIND HARLEYS (AS BEFORE)
Rocket launcher fires. Trees by roadside fireball as Cadillac whips around a bend. GRENADE BIKER zooms ahead.

MEDIUM WIDE SHOT, LOOKING OUT THROUGH
DRIVER'S SIDE WINDOW
SPENCER is still driving car. GRENADE BIKER pulls up beside Cadillac, grins evilly as he one-hands a grenade and pulls pin with teeth.

AMBERLEA and GL blast him at the same instant.

PAN TO:
MEDIUM WIDE SHOT, LOOKING OVER CADILLAC'S
BACK
GRENADE BIKER's Harley wipes out, grenade clatters to highway and explodes, taking out MACHINE-GUN BIKER coming up behind. MAN WITH ROCKET LAUNCHER keeps coming.

SHOT FROM BEHIND HARLEYS (AS BEFORE)

Rocket launcher fires again, just misses Cadillac.

TRACKING SHOT, FROM ABOVE—FRONT OF CAR AND
ROAD BEHIND (AS BEFORE)

AL

I got this.

AL takes big bottle of olive oil from food cooler.

AL (CONT'D)

No salad tonight though.

AL pours oil out side of car, all over the road, then
tosses his cigar after it. Behind, a sheet of flame ignites
as sidecar bike hits the oil and goes into a skid.

Cadillac goes around a curve.

HORN BLARES

SPENCER swerves, and a huge logging truck barrels
around the bend, going the other way.

SOUND OF HUGE CRASH AS TRUCK HITS THE WIPED-
OUT BIKE.

SLOW MOTION:

Through the air, the rocket launcher comes spinning
end over end, over the rocks and lands in the Cadillac,
between AMBERLEA and AL. AMBERLEA grabs it
and aims up and back as the helicopter swoops in on
another run.

                    AMBERLEA
          (aiming up with rocket launcher)
     Steady…

SHOT FROM BEHIND CADILLAC (AS BEFORE)

Track of machine-gun fire pocks the road, getting closer
and closer to the back of the car as AMBERLEA aims.

                    AMBERLEA (CONT'D)
     Now.

AMBERLEA fires.

AMBERLEA'S POINT OF VIEW FROM CAR

Direct hit on helicopter. It fireballs and disintegrates in midair.

TRACKING SHOT, FROM ABOVE—FRONT OF CAR AND ROAD BEHIND (AS BEFORE)

AL

Time for lunch.

GL

Time for a Dependable.

MEDIUM WIDE SHOT FROM SIDE OF ROAD

Wreckage of last bike is crushed beneath wheels of logging truck. Trailer has tipped, spilling logs across the road. Little puddles of burning oil flicker. A black Lincoln Navigator with tinted windows slowly rolls up to the wreckage and stops where the road is blocked.

TWENTY

I know. You don't have to say it. But it would be cool, huh?

What really happens is, Al blows up the outhouse. In the morning, just before we go, there's a lineup for the bathroom, so Al fires up a cigar and heads for the outdoor biffy. He steps in, puffing hard.

"Those things stink." AmberLea wrinkles her nose at the cigar as she watches from the kitchen window. She is not a happy camper this morning. Then again, neither am I. It's ridiculously early and, except for school days, getting up before noon is against my religion.

"He said it smells a lot sweeter than what's in there," I tell her.

"I don't want to find out," she says. Then she calls out, "Hurry up, Gramma! Are you almost done?"

Maybe ten minutes later we've locked the cottage and we're all rolling up the lane in the Cadillac when behind us comes this muffled *boom*, and a *whoosh* that sets the leaves on the trees flapping. I actually feel a blast of air hit the back of my head, and then *clunk*! We all flinch as this chunk of green painted wood with a door hinge on it bounces off the hood of the car. Then more wood and shingles and stuff come crashing down around us. We all shout and swear (well, it's mostly GL) like we're in an R-rated movie, and I almost drive us into the bush. I hit the brakes and we all look back. The roof and door have blown off the outhouse and what's left is on fire. A plume of smoke is already floating above the trees.

"Damn," says GL. "That'll come out of the selling price. Oh well, it's a knockdown anyway."

Al says, "What the—?" Then he looks at his hand and back and his eyes get big. "Did I—? I think I left my cigar in there."

GL shakes her head. "That'll do it. Methane gas. You're lucky you didn't go up too." She settles back in her seat and waves a hand. "Come on, Scooter; nothing we can do now. Let's hit it."

Somewhere a siren is wailing as I ease out onto the road. I guess we're all a little shaken up, because none of us notices I've turned the wrong way until a little way along, when a pickup truck whips past us, going the other way, green lights flashing from its dashboard. I know from going to Grandpa's cottage that green lights mean the driver is a volunteer fire-fighter. I can guess where he's headed.

"Shouldn't we be over the railroad tracks by now?" AmberLea asks.

She's right. I pull over and do my second three-point turn in the Caddy just before a car zooms past with more green lights flashing. I pull over to let another one go by before we get past the cottage again. By now there's a lot of smoke above the trees. I can feel us all trying not to look at it.

Then we're bumping back across the railroad tracks. The siren gets louder. We pass the church, and now I can tell the sound comes from a tower behind the community center. A whole whack of cars and trucks with flashing green lights are back there too, parked every which way. Men are pulling on firefighter suits as a red pumper truck backs out of a garage.

"There you go," says GL. "They'd have hosed you down in no time, Al."

I hear a weak laugh from the backseat as we roll on. Maybe now isn't the time to mention something else I see as we pass: behind the community center, trapped in the middle of all the cars and trucks with the flashing green lights, is a black Lincoln Navigator with tinted windows.

TWENTY-ONE

By now I'm Mr. Confusion. I'm still going with it, but both Grandpa and GL sending me—or us—to Jackfish is too much of a coincidence. And how did the SUV already get here if we shook them yesterday? It's got to be a script. If it is, it's awfully complicated though. Who worked it all out? Was the outhouse rigged to blow up? What about the fancy gunshot that put the hole in the windshield? And why would Grandpa want me to go to Jackfish anyway, even without Gloria Lorraine? Was something else planned for up there? Maybe not, if the deal was to film a road and a deserted town and make up my own story.

On the other hand, all I was supposed to do was get a kiss on the cheek from an old lady. All this other stuff is way too complicated. But if it's all for real, it's too…well, it's too much like a movie.

We stop for a break in Pointe au Baril Station. I'm still thinking it over as I check for texts, standing in front of Al while he gets us clean shirts again, which is trickier in a small place. The signal isn't very strong and I keep moving around, which bugs Al, of course. Finally I see there's one from Deb, one from Jer, and one from Bun. Deb's gives me the name of a book about film noir that will help with my questions. Sylvia will get me a copy. Jer's says ok. Bun's says his tattoo hurts and he's still hanging with Jaden and the posse and something about guns. Sounds as if he's making progress with his video game, maybe pulled an all-nighter. I text him back: outhouse exploded tell u later. That will give Bun something to think about when he isn't blasting aliens or leading a gang war in Parkdale or whatever he's doing. Suddenly I really wish I'd gotten the outhouse explosion on camera. Damn.

Then we're driving again and I'm wondering about my own game and how real it is. How can

I find out? I turn it over in my mind as we head up Highway 69 to where it meets 17 just south of Sudbury, and then we go west on 17 through Blind River, Thessalon and a bunch of other places, all the way to Sault Sainte Marie, where GL says we'll stop for the night. If this is all fake, GL is in on it and Al has to be an actor, so they won't tell me anything. That leaves AmberLea. It's worth a try; she was more talkative last night at the cottage—at least until I bombed out by asking about her house arrest. After we get checked into a Comfort Inn, GL mixes martinis for herself and Al, and they start talking about Vegas. I say to AmberLea, "We should take Mister Bones for a walk."

AmberLea doesn't look any happier than she did this morning, but this might be my only chance. She clips the lead onto Mister Bones's collar and we start down the street. It feels good to stretch my legs. Mister Bones likes it too, hitting two telephone poles and sniffing up a storm. I make a lame joke about phone poles being safer than outhouses. She laughs, and I wish I looked as if I needed a shave. Girls like scruffy guys. I've decided she really is better-looking than I thought at first. I go for it while she's still in a good mood. "You know last night, when you said,

'What's going on?'" Right away she frowns. I keep on anyway. "Well, what *is* going on? Is this for real, do you think? Like Al being a gangster and bad guys chasing us with GPS and stuff?"

AmberLea pushes her sunglasses up to the top of her head and looks at me, hard. I notice she has green eyes before I look away. "You're asking *me*?" she says. "Look, Spinner—"

"Spencer."

"Sorry. Spencer. Whoever. Sorry, all the names she uses get me confused. You're asking the wrong person. I mean, I don't even know who *you* are. I don't know *where* we are. All I know is, you show up yesterday and my gramma drags me off to 'change my life,' and I'm gonna be in it so deep when I get back that I'll need a ladder to get back up to the bottom." She swears and tugs Mister Bones away from a Big Mac wrapper.

Oh, boy. I tell her about Grandpa's will and having to get the kiss and going to Erie Estates and what happened before we picked her up. As I do, her eyes go from blank and angry to confused and angry. "That's weird," she says. "Gramma called the day before yesterday, said she'd be coming over to our house Friday morning and would Mom be around. I said no, because Mom always golfs on Fridays, and she laughed her cackly little laugh and said, 'Perfect, see you then,' and I forgot about it until you all showed up in the Cadillac."

"Well, it gets weirder," I say. "Last night she told us we're going to Jackfish, right? Look at this. It's from my grandpa, about what I was supposed to do if your grandma wasn't around." I give her assignment number two. She reads it and looks at me, even more confused. "So, what's up with Jackfish?" I say. "What's it got to do with her?"

AmberLea shrugs. "Who knows? She's from Kansas. Why did she hide that locket behind a moose head—"

"Deer head."

"Whatever, in a cabin—"

"Cottage."

"*Whatever*—cottage—no one ever knew she had?"

"Well, see, that's what I mean. Maybe it's all a setup. Maybe the cottage was rented. Maybe she got somebody to put a locket behind the deer head. Your grandma is rich, right? She could hire somebody to— well, it could be done."

AmberLea's chin has been tucking in ever since I started talking. Now she's shaking her head. "No. No. First, she isn't rich. My mom says she doesn't have a dime. Her last husband went bankrupt and wiped her out, and the gangster one before that had everything taken by the government. Nobody knew about the cottage. Second, she told me this morning that the money from selling that cabin or cottage or whatever is going to be mine in her will, if I..."

"If you what?"

"Never mind; it's not important." She bends and scratches at her ankle. She seems to do that a lot, I've noticed. Mister Bones comes over to investigate. "The point is, it must be hers. She wouldn't promise me something fake. She's a pain in the butt, but she's always straight up. So that means the picture must be real too."

I'm not convinced. "Okay, then either somebody does know about the cottage, or there's another mystery, because guess what I saw this morning? That black suv again. It was hemmed in behind all the volunteer fire guys' cars back there in Torrance. How did they know where we were going?"

She looks up at me, dead serious. "Maybe there's another transmitter." She scoops up Mister Bones and starts feeling around his collar. Mister Bones wriggles and then licks her face. Considering what else he's been licking in the last few minutes I don't envy her. "There's nothing there." AmberLea puts the dog back down. He trots over to a lamppost. "So, either they knew about the cottage…"

See? I want to yell.

"…or somebody told them where we were going."

"Who?"

"Not me," says AmberLea. "Not Gramma; she doesn't have a phone. Not Al; he couldn't get a signal last night, remember? That leaves you."

"Well, I didn't tell them! I got a signal down on the dock, but I didn't call them."

"Did you tell anybody?"

"Only my brother. He was my only call last night. He doesn't know any mob guys in Buffalo. He's not even going to tell our parents." I doubt his Fifteenth Street skateboarders or video posse or whatever will be interested either, so I leave them out of it. Bunny can be hard to explain sometimes.

AmberLea shrugs. "I don't know then. But the cottage is real. And the picture is real. I caught her looking at it this morning and I thought she was going to cry. Believe me, Gloria Lorraine never cries. She said she had to show me something that nobody else knew. Right now, I guess I have to believe her."

"But," I said, "it's—I don't know—like a movie or something."

She shrugs again. "Gramma always says it's only a movie if you believe. If you don't, it's just the pictures. And you know what? Even if it's all a crock and they hang me by my toes when I get back, it's still been better than staying home." She looks away and tugs at Mister Bones's leash. "Anyway, we should get back." She pulls down her shades. Then she pulls them up again and looks straight at me. "But promise me something? Promise you'll swear she forced me to come."

"Uh, sure. You got it."

"Thanks, Spencer."

We turn back for the motel.

TWENTY-TWO

The next day we drive. And drive. And drive. And drive. We head north from the Sault. Al drives, AmberLea drives, I drive. GL rides shotgun. We pass tiny places—some I can't even pronounce—and they're getting farther apart. We stop a couple of times for food and gas and to let Mister Bones and us do our thing. Except for trucks, there's not much traffic. I start to see what GL meant about life being a movie without jump cuts—especially a road movie.

GL watches the landscape for a while as it gets rockier and scrubbier. She nibbles some of her crackers. She doesn't say much. Then I see her reach in her pocket and turn off her hearing aid; after that she makes like Mister Bones and pretty much dozes.

AmberLea listens to her iPod. Al tries to get a signal on his phone every so often, then swears in a halfhearted way and wrestles with a map. I can't get a signal on my phone either, so I take out my camera and try a few shots when it's not my turn to drive. I get a good one of AmberLea at the wheel, with her hair whipping out behind her, and one of tiny old GL asleep, all hat and scarf, in the front seat. Al says, "Don't even think about it," when I turn the camera toward him, so instead I get a cool rolling-down-the-highway shot through the windshield. Then I turn around and get on my knees for a shot over the back of the car, of the road unwinding behind us. If this *were* a movie, I think to myself as I try to hold the camera steady, what I'd see right now is a black dot on the road back there, getting bigger until it morphs into the black suv, gaining on us, with the motorcycles, and the helicopter would swoosh overhead. Or there'd be a jump cut to wherever we're going so we could skip all this.

But there isn't. No black suvs or killer bikers either. All we get buzzed by are blackflies (one whacks into my head as I'm kneeling there) and rain, after the Sault. We stop to put the top up and everything seems dark and dreary and even more boring.

At White River, we stop for an early dinner. We stagger into a restaurant you can tell smells permanently of French fries. A lot of rigs are parked outside. I'm guessing the rest of the customers are truckers. The map and gps both tell us we've got about an hour to go to Marathon, where GL says we're going to stop. She's had enough for today.

"Thank god," says Al as we sink into a booth. I nod. I never thought sitting could make me so tired.

AmberLea brings GL back from the restroom and folds her in beside me. You can practically hear GL's hinges creak. She was so stiff when we got out of the car that I wondered if we'd have to unbend her ourselves. She looks wornout, even after her naps. Some of her face powder has come off and her lipstick is blurry and staining her teeth. When the waitress shows up with coffee, she has a cup right off.

"Gramma," AmberLea warns, "you never drink coffee."

145

"It's a special occasion." She hunches over the cup. "I need this like hell needs a fire hose. I used to live on this stuff."

By the time the waitress takes our orders, GL's perked up some. "Between the caffeine and the bathroom I'll be up all night," she says, panting a little, "but right now it's worth it. Now," she goes on, leaning across the table, both hands around her cup, as if she's some moose trapper who's lived up here forever, "Jackfish is on toward Terrace Bay. We'll stop in Marathon tonight, rest up and be there in the morning. Just the way I promised." She looks at us, as if we've been whining all day.

"And what are we going to do in beautiful Jackfish, Gramma?" Two days on the road haven't left AmberLea any too perky either.

"Unfinished business. Believe the living and bury the dead."

"I've heard that before," Al says.

GL nods. "My big line in *Shadow Street*. Just because it's from a movie doesn't mean it isn't true." She looks back to AmberLea. "You'll see tomorrow. A little secret between you and me." She turns to me. "And we can't forget Spike's kiss for his Grandpa David, can we? Then"—she waves a hand like it weighs forty pounds—"Al can hightail it to Grand Portage or Fort Frances and duck into Minnesota if he wants."

"What I want"—Al waves his phone—"is to find out if things have cooled off in Buffalo. I got a business to run."

"And I'm sure it needs all those baking supplies in the trunk," says GL. "Maybe you'd like to drive us back then. You can thank us for saving you when you say goodbye."

"Yeah, how do we get back?" I say. "You told me to say we'd be home tomorrow."

"I may have been a little hasty on that," says GL. She nods to the rest of the room. "On the other hand, I'll bet not many of these fine young men would turn down a little old lady and her lovely granddaughter if they were hitchhiking. I've done it before."

"*Really?*" says AmberLea. "Gramma! When?"

"When I was your age. If it wasn't the stupidest thing I've ever done, it was close to it." GL pats me on the arm. "I'm sure they'd make room for our personal photographer on the bumper or the trailer hitch. Don't worry, Skeezix; just kidding. If Al doesn't want to go back, we can easily get a bus ticket. Or we could just get a cab."

Before I can even begin to wonder if she's kidding, the waitress arrives with the food and GL digs out all her pills as the food is put down. When the waitress leaves, GL says, "Screen me." She empties her water glass into the pot of plastic plants behind the booth; then out comes the gin bottle from her straw bag, under the table. She glugs some gin into the glass and whisks the bottle back into the bag as the waitress comes by with ketchup. "If you have to take pills," says GL, "it might as well be fun." She gets down to it.

She's a little wobbly on the way out to the car. Once she's in, she settles herself as if she's dozing again. But I'm driving, and from the side I can see behind her sunglasses. She's watching every inch of the way.

TWENTY-THREE

Not long before we get to Marathon, GL stirs herself. She roots around in her bag and gets busy fixing her makeup. Then she insists we pull over and put the top down on the car. "I want to make an entrance," she says.

"To Marathon?" AmberLea says.

"Indulge me. I'm an old lady."

There's no real reason why not; it's still a bright, sunny evening, even if it's cooling off. Down goes the top. GL settles her hat and gets a cigarette pose going. We roll into town in style: a ninety-year-old bombshell, a blond ankle-scratcher with a vanishing chin,

Buffalo's King of Cannoli, a Chihuahua and a movie-geek chauffeur with bent glasses and a big need for a shower, all in a dented white Cadillac with stolen plates, a bullet hole, five big bags of something that might be icing sugar, and its own helium supply. It's not four gunslingers riding into town, but it might be the closest I'll get.

"Damn," says GL, as we roll past two kids bending over a skateboard and a guy checking his tire pressure. "We should have had the car washed."

"It rained while you were asleep," Al reminds her. "We're good."

"Oh. All right then." She gives a queenly smile to a golden retriever in the back of a pickup truck. Mister Bones yaps.

We pick the Superior Motel because it's the first one we see and it looks okay. "You can always tell about motels," Al advises. "You wanna lie low, pick one's gotta car with a flat parked at a unit."

"Why?" I ask.

"Car with a flat says cash, cheap and close."

"Close?"

"To your basics. You know, like a liquor store."

"How do you know that?"

"If you hadda drive, you'd fix the flat."

Al and I go into the motel office. There's a big, fleshy-faced old guy in saggy jeans and a black golf shirt behind the desk. The only thing even close to being as big as his gut is his huge upsweep of silver hair. It curves out over his forehead, then rolls and swoops straight to the back of his head, kind of like young Elvis, except old.

Over in the corner an even older guy is parked on a couch, dozing in front of a TV blaring CNN. He's all wrinkles and stray whiskers under his ball cap, and he's got the belt-and-suspenders combo happening over green work pants and a plaid shirt.

Al pulls out a credit card and books two rooms while I look around. I'm tired and this place isn't making me feel any livelier. There are fake flowers here too, and potted palm trees, a rack of postcards and some tour brochures.

On the wall behind the desk, on a wooden plaque, is a big stuffed fish with its mouth wide open and some framed photos—pictures of kids' soccer teams wearing *Superior Motel* jerseys, grad shots, a wedding,

---

old people with a cake and party hats. That kind of stuff. Underneath hang plaques and certificates from the Chamber of Commerce and the Rotary Club. Jer once had to give a speech about "Front Porch Farmer" to a Rotary Club. I look closer at the inscription. The name on the plaque reads *Mike Karpuski.* Why does that sound familiar?

To one side are three black-and-white pictures. One is of a bunch of guys on a dock, in old-fashioned clothes, squinting into the sun and holding up a big fish; another is a line of people standing in front of a plain wooden building with a sign above their heads: *Superior Hotel.* Then I jolt out of my tiredness, because the third picture is different. First of all, it's been torn into pieces and carefully taped back together. Second, I've seen it before. It's a soft focus, head-and-shoulders glamour shot of a platinum blond, one dark eyebrow arched knowingly at the camera. At the bottom, on the right, perfect handwriting flows: *Best wishes always, Gloria Lorraine.*

"Hey," I say.

Al doesn't notice. He's busy stuffing whatever hot credit card he used back into a wallet. The guy behind the desk is handing over two keys on plastic tags.

"One-twelve and one-fourteen there, Mr. Scrimger," he rumbles over the din from the TV. "Halfway down the west side. You can park right in front. Enjoy your stay."

Al scoops up the keys. "Sure we will. C'mon, Ed. Let's get Gramma settled."

I follow him out. "Did you see that?" I ask him. "It was so weird."

"See what? Was somethin' on the news?"

"No, on the wall!" We're at the car. "Guess what?" I say to GL as we get in. "You have fans here with the same name as your alias."

"Not now, Spicer." She's tilted onto the door's armrest. It looks as if her grand entrance has used up whatever energy she had left. Her left hand moves to turn off her hearing aid. I stop her. "No, listen, you'll like this. Remember how you had the cottage sign marked *Karpuski* for privacy? That must be the name of the people who run this place, because there's this award on the wall for a Mike Karpuski. And they have one of your old pictures up there too! How weird is that?"

Gloria Lorraine straightens up. Her eyes flare and water for a second as she stares through the damaged windshield. She takes a deep breath, reaches up, snaps down the sun visor and checks herself out in the mirror. Then she opens the car door. "Help me in," she says.

TWENTY-FOUR

We all go. I hold the door while AmberLea helps GL totter inside. Al cradles Mister Bones. The TV is still blaring. When she gets through the door, GL shakes AmberLea off her arm and straightens up as best she can. Then, with just her cane, she almost sashays over to the desk.

"Can I help you?" The big guy with the big hair puts down some papers and takes off a pair of half-glasses.

GL doesn't answer for a long moment; she's checking out the wall display behind him. She stares at her taped-together photo, then steadies herself against the desk. She arches one eyebrow and does her best Gloria Lorraine: "I'm told there's a Mike… Karpuski here."

"You're talking to him," says the guy.

GL shakes her head. "You're too young."

If he's young, I'm Santa Claus, I think, but the guy just chuckles and says, "Oh, you want Big Mike. That's my dad. I'm Little Mike. That's Big Mike over there." He nods at the snoozer by the TV.

GL turns stiffly and looks at Big Mike. His jaw and his ball cap have both come adrift as he slumps on the couch. I notice his fly has wandered a little too, and under the TV noise he's snoring a little. GL's chin starts to tremble. Then she bunches her lips together in a thin red line and starts across the room, leaning on her cane. AmberLea trails her hesitantly. "Turn that…" GL waves at the TV, never taking her eyes off the old guy. AmberLea finds the button.

In the sudden silence, the guy at the desk says, "He had a stroke last year, ma'am. It can be hard talking to him. There's a lot he's not clear about."

I can't tell if GL hears him or not. AmberLea helps her sit down beside Big Mike. Slowly, GL reaches out and touches the old man's arm. "Mikey," she whispers.

"Mikey." Then she's talking in a foreign language; I don't know what it is. "Mikey," she says again, gently shaking his arm, then more foreign language, then, "It's Wandi."

The old man jerks a little and his eyes open. "Gone," he says, or maybe it's "gun." It's hard to tell. He looks blearily at GL.

She says, "I was gone, Mikey. Now I'm back."

"Wandi?" croaks the old man. "You look bad. You been sick?"

She clutches his hand. "I'm old, Mikey. We're both old."

He nods. "It's late, isn't it? You stay here. I'll get you something. Papa will be mad if he finds out, but he never finds out, does he? He was very mad, Wandi. But Mama will be happy. She cried and cried. She'll help in the morning and be happy."

GL nods. "It's okay, Mikey. I can get it myself. You go back to sleep. I'll see you in the morning and we'll talk then."

"Okay. I'm glad you're back, Wandi."

"Me too." She leans forward and gives him a kind of hug. His knobbly hand comes off his lap far enough to pat her back. Then she struggles to her feet, leaning hard on her cane and the sofa back. "Night night, Mikey," she says. "Sleep tight." She lifts a hand off the sofa back and pats his shoulder; then she lifts his cap and plants a kiss on his forehead. "See you in the morning."

The old man's eyes close again. GL makes her way back to the desk. AmberLea moves in to help her. We're all staring. Little Mike is leaning forward, mouth open, both hands on the countertop. "Are—?" he starts to say, but GL cuts him off, stabbing with her cane at the damaged glossy on the wall.

"I'm Gloria Lorraine," she says. "I'm also your Aunt Wanda, and this is your second cousin, AmberLea."

TWENTY-FIVE

"Is that camera ready?" says GL. "It better be, because I've only got one take in me."

She's propped up on a flowery couch. Her feet don't reach the ground, but that's okay; they won't be in the shot. We've moved a couple of lamps for extra light.

"My left side, don't forget. Get left profile and full face; no right side. Move the lamp more that way!"

I'm setting up the camera on its little collapsible tripod.

"Right beside you," she says, "so I look at you, not the camera. More natural."

We're all in the living room of Little Mike's house, up behind the parking lot. It feels empty. It turns out Mike has three kids, all grown and gone, and right now his wife is away visiting her own mom in a nursing home. Big Mike has been helped off to bed, and the night clerk is on at the motel. Little Mike has rustled up snacks for us and glasses of scotch for Al and GL. "This is wild," he says, slowly shaking his head. "I think I knew Pop had a sister who went away a long time ago, but I'm not even sure how I knew. Whispers, I guess. The whole thing was out of bounds, especially around Grandpop and Baba."

"I guess nobody mentioned the money I sent Mikey every month, as soon as I could afford it," GL says drily.

"Well, I'll tell you," says Little Mike, "money was tight when I was a kid, but somehow there was a nest egg waiting to send me to university. The day I left, Pop said, 'Don't thank me, thank your aunt.' So I asked who my aunt was, and he laughed and said, 'She's a movie star.' He had your picture on the wall with a few other celebrity types that had come to the old place for the hunting and fishing. I didn't take him seriously; I figured he was just being modest, sorta deflecting the praise from himself, you know? He's that kind of guy."

"He was a sweet boy." GL nods. "I'm glad the money helped."

"I owe you one," Little Mike says, raising his glass. "A late thanks."

"Cheers."

"Gramma," AmberLea cuts in, from a chair beside Al. "You were born in Topeka, Kansas!" Her chin has had time to reappear, but she's scratching her ankle like mad. "And your family moved to—"

"I know, Washington State. Claptrap. Studio fairy tale." GL waves her hand. "The PR department at Republic made that up to turn me into an all-American girl. Kansas was big that year. Thank *The Wizard of Oz*. They lied about my age too; made me four years younger."

"But Mom—"

GL cuts her off. "Your mother doesn't know anything about this. Nobody does, because I've never told anyone before. I'm doing this for you, AmberLea, and for David McLean."

Grandpa. I look up from plugging in the adaptor. "And for Spencer." GL nods at me. "If it weren't for you, none of this would have happened. I have to tell you about David too, if you're going to understand."

I can't believe it—not just about Grandpa, but that she finally got my name right. "We're ready to go," I say.

"Good. Let's do it. Quiet, everybody. Give me a finger count in."

I raise my right hand, three fingers up. "Three... two...one...go."

I press the button. GL starts her big scene.

TWENTY-SIX

"The first time I saw your grandfather," says GL, "it was 1935. I was seventeen and he was fifteen, I'm guessing. How we all got this old is beyond me. Anyway, he was yelling in the dining room—if you could call it that—of the Superior Hotel in Jackfish. The hotel was my family's—the Karpuski's—business. My father and my Uncle Pete ran it, and we all worked there. We did all right too, especially after we got beer in. Twenty-five cents a bottle; expensive because we had to ship it in, of course. Jackfish was busy, and we were the only game in town. There was a coal dock and stop for the railroad, a little fishing fleet, and for a year or two they were building the North Shore highway past us and the work crews all came in.

"I cleaned rooms, cooked—god, I was a terrible cook; it's a wonder someone didn't die—but mostly Mama cooked and I waited table, and even little Mikey swept and bussed. The dining room had long wooden tables with benches that would fill up with working men. When we first opened, the tables were planks on sawhorses.

"A waitress didn't need much memory back then; there wasn't much on the menu: stew, fish, corned-beef hash, ham and eggs. What you needed was strong arms, an armor-plate ass—they'd pinch your backside every chance they got—and a temperament to take the kidding, because there was a lot of it. I could give it right back, as good as I got, but my father didn't like me to. He wanted to keep me away from men, and I'd already decided I liked them.

"What the hell he wanted to keep me *for* was anybody's guess. It was the middle of the Depression and we were a million miles from nowhere. We argued enough about it then, and sometimes more than argued. He raised his hand to me and to Mama, and to Mikey, more than once. Anyway, it didn't matter:

he didn't know I was already crazy in love with a boy, Danny Gernsbach, an American from Michigan, who worked on the fishing boats. And I didn't know that I was already carrying Danny's child, though I figured it out soon enough.

"One Saturday night, one of the road crews came in for supper, their big night out in town, because they were in camp through the week. I didn't notice Davey at first; it was busy and road crews were always a mixed bag anyway. Besides, Danny and the other fellas from his boat were there too, and I only had eyes for him. God, he was a sweet boy: high, wide and handsome.

"Anyway, the old hands on the road crew had a trick they'd play on the new guys, for initiation, I guess. The tables were covered with oilcloths that dropped over the sides. They'd curl the dropped part up to make a trough under the table. Someone at the end would pour water into it and they'd send it down into the lap of the new man, who wouldn't see it coming. Then he'd yell, of course, and jump up and make a fuss. Some would be angry and some would laugh and some wouldn't know what to do. But how you handled it put you in or out.

"Well, that night I was coming round with the coffeepot and I saw them start the trough and wink at me, and a second later there's a shriek just like a girl's and a big roar of laughter, and there's your grandpa, leaping to his feet looking like he's just wet himself. And naturally, they're all watching to see what he's going to do after that shriek. Except he was just a kid, and you could see he didn't *know* what to do. He flushed to the roots of his hair and, I swear to god, for a second I thought he was going to cry—which would not have been a good idea, let me tell you. He was big, you understand, but all at once he just looked like this little child among all these rough men. Maybe it reminded me of Mikey, I don't know, but my heart just went out to him. I didn't know my own troubles yet. All I could think to do was toss him the dishtowel I had over my shoulder, wave the coffeepot and call to him, 'They must like you. If they don't, they do it with this!' My first ad lib, and it brought the house down, if I do say so myself.

"And to give Davey credit—this was how I first knew he was special—he managed to pull himself together while they all laughed, and then he topped it. He slapped on a grin and said, 'But if they *really* like you, I bet it's beer!' and that brought the house down again and he was in.

"Well, later he thanked me and it got so that every once in a while at night he'd sneak down from the camp and talk to me at the kitchen door. I knew he was sweet on me, but I felt like his big sister, and besides, I was crazy for Danny. David was just a kid and I could tell he was still scared and lonely up here, doing the best he could. Once my father caught me talking to him and chased him off and then smacked me, but even that was good, because it kept him from suspecting about Danny.

"And then it all went south. I found out I was in the family way. I told Danny and he said we'd get married, right away, down in Michigan. And he meant it too. He was a good boy. He sent a wire home, saying we were coming. But we never went: Danny's boat went out the next morning and there was an accident. He got tangled in a net and he drowned. They brought him back and buried him in the Jackfish graveyard.

"I thought I was going to die too, of grief for Danny and for me with this baby, and I couldn't show it. I couldn't tell Mama, though there was something, maybe just the way she looked at me, that told me she knew anyway. But I couldn't take the risk, couldn't have her involved. If my father had found out, there would have been no telling what he'd have done.

"Well, in the middle of all that, one night Davey came to the kitchen door, all excited. He said something about how he'd seen a plane flying over that morning and now he knew what he wanted to do: he wanted to fly. I was trying to keep everything in, but he saw I'd been crying and he stopped and asked what was wrong and it all came spilling out. The first thing he said was—and this is the kind of man he must have grown up to be—the first thing he said was, 'I'll marry you.'

"I can still see him there, looking in at me, his hands on the screen door, a big kid with big eyes. I don't think he even needed to shave yet. I said, 'Davey, that's awful sweet, but you're not even sixteen. You can't marry me, and it wouldn't be right anyway.' And he said, 'Well, what are you going to do?' And I said, 'I don't know, but I have to get away from here. I can't stay.' Because, I think, as soon as he'd said he was going to·fly, at that moment I'd made up my mind to go. How I was going to do it, I had no idea.

I had no money and no place to go, but now that I'd said it, I knew it was what I had to do.

"The next night, Davey was back at the kitchen door. He'd gotten an advance on his pay and he gave me everything he'd saved, all of it. He said I needed it more that he did. We both knew there was a west-bound express that made a coaling stop in Jackfish after midnight. He promised he'd be at the station to see me off, and then he was gone.

"I put a few things in a little overnight case some guest had left behind. I kissed Mikey goodbye, even though he was sound asleep, and I slipped out. I waited in the shadows on the platform till the last second, but Davey never came. As we pulled out, I thought I saw someone running, but it was too late; I never got to give him a thank-you kiss goodbye.

"Davey's money got me away. In Saskatoon, I bought a wedding ring in a pawnshop for seventy-five cents and wore it as soon as I started to show. I said I was Mrs. Danny Gernsbach. No one believed me when I said I was a widow, even though I thought I truly was. They all thought I was just another tramp who got what was coming to her. When the baby was born, a little girl, I called her Danielle.

They all tried to persuade me to put her up for adoption, but I couldn't let her go.

"Somehow I got Dani and me out to Vancouver, and then down to Seattle. I got a job slinging hash in a luncheonette there. I rented a room and the landlady looked after Dani sometimes and sometimes I took her to work.

"But there was never enough money, even for proper food, even working at a lunch counter. Everyone was scraping by. Dani took sick and I had to quit work to look after her. The medicine was expensive and so was the doctor. I did some things I'm not proud of...But the medicine didn't help and Danielle died anyway. The next week I was wiping the counter at the luncheonette and wondering what the best way was to kill myself, when a fat man with an ugly tie came in and looked at me and said, 'Turn to your right.' I was in such a daze that I did it and just went on wiping. Then he said, 'Kid, how'd you like to be in pictures?' And that was the way I chose to kill Wanda Karpuski.

"As soon as I could, I started sending money to Mikey, along with that picture. Looks like my father got a hold of that. I never saw or spoke with any of them again, and I've never had a good man in love with me since. I used up my quota in Jackfish. I tried to come back, but the closest I got was buying that cabin on Lake Muskoka. Even that was too close, so I rented it out. I had no idea David was right across the lake.

"And I never thought I'd come back, until my granddaughter got as headstrong as I did and a young man asked me for a kiss, David's kiss. Then I knew we were going to come here. So tomorrow we'll finish things off. I'm here so she can help me to put a picture of his daughter on Danny's grave. Then I'm going to give Spencer the kiss on the cheek that David never got. Then I'll be done with it all."

TWENTY-SEVEN

The room stays quiet after Gloria Lorraine stops talking. Nobody moves. After a moment I hit the Stop button and GL sags in the couch. "You didn't say 'Cut,'" she whispers. Then AmberLea is beside her, holding her.

I go outside. It's clouded over, but still not dark. The streetlights and the SUPERIOR MOTEL sign have come on though. I don't know what to think, except, It's all true. Which means, among other things, that we really were chased by mobsters. Almost out of habit, I look up and down the highway: no black Lincoln Navigators. That all seems a million years ago anyway.

I'm not sure what to feel either, except sad, somehow, and confused. To keep from thinking and feeling anymore, I swat away a couple of insects and check my cell for messages. I have to walk around to get a signal. Finally, down near the motel sign, I do. First I text Bun: almost dun. Jackfish ghost town tomorrow morning. There's another message from Deb, suggesting a restaurant in New York that Gloria Lorraine might like, near the AFI, which I know means American Film Institute. Maybe Jer will tell me what GL and I were doing there. My guess is some kind of interview. Jer has been spinning this one hard. I have to admit it's not how I thought he'd take me disappearing off the face of the earth. Speaking of which, I wonder where *he* is. Maybe he's in New York, faking it for us.

The signal has disappeared. I move toward the parking lot and get it back. I text Jer: thanx. Then I text him again: dun mon am. can u meet in Marathon ON Superior motel or I go to Buf? Now that it's almost over, it won't hurt to tell, and besides, it doesn't sound like there's a game plan yet for getting home. I wonder if he can get here by Monday morning from wherever he is.

It's not really like asking for a ride home from the mall. But right now it's too much to wonder about.

That night I sleep in one of Little Mike's kids' rooms. I dream Jer and I are driving in the Caddy and the black suv is catching up to us and no matter how hard I step on the gas we don't go any faster. What makes it scarier is that somehow I know Grandpa is driving the suv, except that he's also with us in the Cadillac and he's going to pour something in my lap and I don't know if it's beer or coffee.

Let's just say it's a weird night.

TWENTY-EIGHT

Monday morning comes early. It's cloudy and gray, and it feels as if I haven't slept at all. In the kitchen, Al is talking retail baking with Little Mike. They trade business cards. "I'll be in touch," says Al. "I know local works for you, but if we go national, you might want a few specialty items, you know?"

I have a piece of toast with peanut butter, make sure the camera is charged and wander outside with it and Mister Bones. AmberLea is stowing GL's cooler in the trunk of the car, with the helium tank and all the bags of white powder.

"So," I say, "today's the day."

She nods. I guess neither of us really knows what to say. I don't anyway. AmberLea says, "I won't be sorry to change my clothes. I wonder how we're getting home. What do you think Al will do?"

"I dunno. I texted my dad last night and asked him for a ride. He could probably take you and GL too."

"Oh. Good. Thanks." She sighs. "I wonder what my mom is doing—besides freaking." She pulls her phone out of her back pocket. I have completely rethought my position on her and tight jeans. They're a definite plus. AmberLea waves her phone. "There's about a million texts from her on here. I haven't even looked at them. I'm kind of scared to."

"Your grandma will look after it. She said she would, remember?"

"It's not that simple."

"Well," I say, "you can't answer them now. The signal up here keeps disappearing. And anyway"—I wipe my peanut-buttery fingers on my jeans—"we have to get to Jackfish."

Al and Little Mike come out of the house, helping GL. "You're sure you remember the way?" Mike is saying. GL is nodding.

"Okay," Mike says, "but it won't look the same. It's all overgrown now. Be careful walking. And don't try for the town. Since the fire, it's pretty grim. If you really want to go in there, I could take you in on the ATV."

"I don't want the town," says GL, "I want the graveyard."

Little Mike looks at Al and me and AmberLea. "Just be careful. I'd feel a lot better if you let me come along."

"I have to do this myself," says GL. "I'm a Jackfish girl. We'll be back for lunch. Anyway, this isn't your affair."

"It's my family," says Mike.

GL eyes him. She nods. "I'll give you that one. But I'm doing this my way."

Mike sighs and smoothes one side of his silver 'do. "Fair enough. Tell you what. I've got to run over to Terrace this morning anyway, so follow me along to the Jackfish road now and I'll meet you up at the top by the highway at, say, eleven thirty."

"Done and done," says GL. "Let's go."

We drive with the top up, following Mike west on Highway 17. Al is at the wheel and I'm riding shotgun, with AmberLea and GL in the back. Nobody says much. For half an hour, rock and trees and a couple of sort of villages roll by us, a few bugs whack the windshield, and then, up ahead, Little Mike's arm is pointing left out his window, and there's a road sign, green and white, reading *Jackfish Road*. This is it.

Al slows the Caddy as Mike rolls on, and we take the left after a transport truck roars by. We're on a gravel road now. Stones grind and click off the bottom of the car. Inside, we're silent. I glance into the back. GL has her hand locked in AmberLea's.

We pass a little white sign that says *Municipal Landfill*. AmberLea breaks the quiet. "Is that a *bear*?" I look toward the dump, but before I spot anything, the Cadillac has crested a hill and on the right is a lake.

"Jackfish Lake," GL croaks.

A little farther on, the bush on either side of the road gives way to a big empty clearing. There are a couple of piles of gravel and stacks of ancient logs and railroad ties. A tired old Honda Civic rests by one of the piles. It could have been there for an hour or a hundred years. Across the bottom of the clearing runs a railroad track, with a line of graffiti-covered freight cars sitting on it. "Pull in here," says GL. "Go over to the east side." Her voice has gotten higher and sharper.

Al eases the Caddy across the ruts toward the deep woods and brings us to a stop, still well away from the trees. "That's as far as I can get us," he says.

"Then we walk from here," announces GL.

"Where?" asks AmberLea. Looking back, I see her chin has disappeared as she stares at the bush.

"Along the railroad tracks," says GL.

"Is that safe?"

"It's just a siding. We only have to go a little way on the main line." GL says this as if any fool should know it. "Open the trunk," she says. "Let's go."

Al pops the trunk. The insects start buzzing as soon as we get out of the car.

"Get me that bag." GL snaps her fingers at her plastic bag in the trunk. She pulls out bottles of insect repellent. "Be generous with yourself."

We all start slapping the stuff on. It's incredibly rank and scummy feeling, but it seems to work. Now the bugs just swarm and buzz and dive without ever quite biting. I think of Grandpa's Marauding Mosquitoes. I look into the bag, hoping she's brought hazmat suits or something—even hats. Instead, she's got garden gloves, trimmers and a tin of white spray paint in there.

"What's that stuff for?"

"When we find the grave, we're going to tidy it up. We'll paint the cross."

"Find the grave? Don't you—?"

"First we have to find the cemetery. Come on."

"*Find* the cemetery?"

"It's been seventy-five years since my last visit. If you don't hustle it's going to be another seventy-five before we get there. Get your camera and hurry up; I don't have that long."

Al gives me the keys. I dive back into the Caddy, grab the video camera and lock the car again. Then off we start for the tracks, dripping insect repellent and helping GL over the uneven ground. Mister Bones trots all over the place. GL is right: at this rate it'll take us another seventy-five years— if we don't get eaten by bears or flattened by a train first. Luckily we're equipped with spray paint, grass clippers, phones with no signals and a Chihuahua; everything you need when you're looking for the graveyard of a ghost town in the northern bush.

TWENTY-NINE

But wait, it gets worse. We're just going around a pile of railroad ties, almost at the tracks, when we hear a low rumble. It gets louder, then deafening, and for a second I wonder if a train is rolling in. Then two men on giant motorcycles roll into the clearing, their choppers blatting and farting like hungover moose. They pull up and look around. Instinctively, we all duck behind the railroad ties. The engines cut out. In the tingly silence that comes after, a voice gripes, "I haven't felt my bleeping butt since Wawa."

"Nobody wants to bleeping feel your bleeping butt anyway," says another voice.

"Bleep bleep smart guy bleep."

They didn't really say *bleep*, but I'm hoping to keep this mostly PG. I peek around the railroad ties as they get off their bikes. They're big guys in biker boots, leather pants and sleeveless jean jackets. One guy has a huge droopy mustache to go with his gut. The other is short, but as wide as he is tall. His head is a helmet with an orange beard exploding out the bottom. Al is a big guy. These two make him look like a carrot stick, and me a cardboard match, or worse.

"Think that's it?" Mustache says. "Looks like they ditched it."

"Gotta bleeping be," says Beard. "This is bleeping Jackfish and that's a bleeping white Caddy."

"The stuff better be in there. Let's find out and get outta here." They're waving away the bugs as they look around the clearing. As they turn, I see the backs of their jean jackets feature a big capital letter *A* with a circle over it, like a halo, maybe. I duck back, then peek again as their boots crunch toward Al's car. Beside me, Al is moaning softly, "Aw no, no!"

"Who are they?" I hiss.

"They must be the bikers that were part of the deal," Al hisses back. "I told ya: it's some kind of three-way setup: the Wings, some street gang and bikers. I was supposed to pick up drugs for Rocco and his boys to deliver. Word was, they were going to deal 'em to this whaddyacallit—*posse*, that's it— outta state, so *they* could deal the stuff to bikers for god knows what; guns, I think. Something like that anyway. But if these are the bikers, how did they know to come here?"

I look carefully over the woodpile. Mustache is yanking at a door handle. "Let's do the top," he growls. He pulls something from a pocket, flicks it, and there's the biggest knife I've ever seen.

"Nah," Orange Beard says, "I'll get it." He raises one gigantic biker-booted foot and kicks the trunk lock with his heel. *CLUNK.* A big dent creases the white metal, way bigger than the ones GL made with her cane back in Buffalo.

"Aw, noooo!" Al again.

"Why don't you just give them the drugs?" AmberLea whispers.

"Because it's *icing sugar*!"

"In a pig's eye," snaps GL. "Cut the crap. Give them the fairy dust and we'll get on with our business. This isn't what we're here for."

CLUNK. "Hurry up. The bugs are nuts here." Sounds like Mustache.

"We don't even have a gun," Al whines. "What did you ditch my gun for?"

"Fat lot of good it would do you anyway," huffs GL.

CLUNK. Over by the car a voice says, "Let's just use the can opener." Then there's a flat *crack,* like the one I heard back in the Buffalo parking lot. Al winces as if he got shot himself.

I peek out again. Orange Beard has a gun in his fist. The trunk lid has popped up a few inches. Both bikers are too busy waving away blackflies to open it all the way yet. As Orange Beard reaches for the lid, a black Lincoln Navigator roars into the clearing, pulling a skid stop that puts it sideways to the bikers. Out the far side tumble the Wings boys, KK and AB, guns drawn across the hood of the suv. "Get away from the car," one of them shouts.

THIRTY

Orange Beard and Mustache have spun around as the suv barrels in. Now they dive behind the Cadillac and they shout back something with a lot of bleeps in it. Then there are five or six cracks and pops. One bullet dings the Cadillac's fender, there's a spurt of gravel near the suv, and I'm pretty sure one shot whangs a tag on a freight car. Who knows where the rest go? Either these guys are hopeless shots or real shooting isn't the way it is in movies and games.

"Oh, for crying out loud," sighs GL, as there's more swearing and shouting. "I've got to sit down if this is going to take long. Help me, Amby."

Then the shouting changes. There's something going on at the suv. AB Wings calls out, "All right, who are you guys?"

There's a pause; then voices come from behind the Cadillac. Orange Beard shouts, "Angels. Mimico Angels. There's something in the car belongs to us. Who are you?"

"Buffalo," calls AB Wings, "and it doesn't belong to you yet."

Beside me, Al gives a quiet little groan.

"Buffalo?" Now AmberLea squints around the far end of the woodpile. "Them? How did *they* get here? You said we lost them in Torrance, when the outhouse blew up."

"*In Torrance*?" Al says. "They were in Torrance? Sheesh, why didn't you tell me?"

"Never mind," I say. "I'll tell you later." I keep on looking out, wondering how *did* they get here?

"It belongs to us now," calls Orange Beard. "This was supposed to go down in Toronto. The posse told us you were here. Why? Somebody's bleeping jerking us around, either you or the posse, and we don't like it. We kept our side of the deal. Now we get what's ours."

"We had a guy go offside on us. He ran it to here. We just got here ourselves."

"Well, you're too bleeping late. It's ours now."

"Not without cash or merchandise."

"Get it from the bleeping posse."

"We'll take it from you."

"Fine. Take it." Another shot cracks out. This one smacks the Navigator's glass behind the back door. The glass doesn't break.

There's quiet while the Wings boys shuffle behind the suv. "Well," says GL, "if that's that, let's just toddle along while they're busy. Help me up." None of us move. I wonder if her hearing aid is on. I find myself taking out my camera.

Then there's a new voice from the clearing, shaking, growling and a thousand years old. "Aww-rii-ight, it's me yuh needa talk ta. I'm Rocco. Lemme tell ya what we're gonna do. Me and my boys here, and youse over there, we're all gonna put our heat on top of the cars and walk out into the middle where we can talk this over sensible, like gennelmen. I'm ninety-years-old an' I don't move fast, so any double cross, I'll be the first ta get it. Come on."

I focus and pan as Rocco Wings starts out from behind the suv. He's still in his red blazer and yellow shirt, and his black hair gleams even brighter than his white shoes. Pushing his walker over the gravel makes him all shaky. You can practically hear his bones rattle. Slowly the others come up from behind the cars. Guns clunk down on metal. "Evvybody keep their hands where evvybody can see 'em," croaks Rocco Wings. "Mine are busy. Vincent, help me heah."

They meet, more or less in the middle. KK Wings helps the old man into the chair seat on his walker. He holds out his gnarly old hand to the bikers. "Rocco Wings."

"We've heard about you, man," says Mustache, shaking hands. "Everybody has. You're a legend." Orange Beard nods in agreement.

"Pleased ta hear it," Rocco Wings says. "So's you know, I deal hard but fair. Awright. The way I see it, we got two things to settle, and the sooner the better. First, we were supposed ta deal merchandise to this what, Possum gang—what are they?"

"Fifteenth Street Posse," says AB Wings.

"Fifteenth Street Posse," repeats Rocco. "And they were supposed to deal to you. Am I right?"

"Right on," says Mustache.

"Okay then. Second, do we need them for a three-way deal or can we do a two?"

They start talking about Toronto and where the money is, and I don't understand any of it. On the other hand, I'm really not trying. Right now I'm getting a very bad feeling, because I just figured out how they found us.

I pull out my phone and scroll through my texts, and there it is: a photo of Bunny's tattoo, a striped number fifteen with a snuffed-out candle beside it. He had said he had to get it to be in the *Fifteenth Street Posse*. Just before he repeated every single thing I told him in that special way of his. How did my brother end up hanging with a street gang who were in a drug deal with the mob and some bikers? Does he even *know* he's hanging with a street gang who are doing a three-way drug deal? Well, I can't deal with that right now. Besides, Bunny handles stuff better than you'd think. And if he can't, there's always Deb. In fact, the posse might not be here because she's enrolled them in a Plato seminar.

This is good, because now I realize we have to deal with something a lot more urgent. Rocco Wings is saying, "…so the posse told us to come heah, but they're not heah. And neither is the one who ran wit' our product."

"Scratch said he was coming," says Orange Beard. "He's posse boss."

"But he don't seem to be here, do he?" crackles Rocco. "Look inna trunk."

KK Wings and Mustache open the trunk. "It's here."

"It better be classic," says Orange Beard.

"It is," says AB Wings. "Guaranteed."

"Sweet," says Orange Beard. "After we step on it, it'll be diet."

They all laugh and then Rocco Wings gets back to business. "If the product is here, then someone else is too. Let's have a look aroun'. This would be a nice quiet place to settle everything."

It's going to take them about ten seconds flat to find us. We have to do something, fast.

"Call nine-one-one," I hiss to AmberLea.

"Don't call nine-one-one," hisses Al.

"I can't anyway," she hisses back. "There's no signal."

"Is that Rocco Wings out there?" says GL. "Let me deal with him."

"No!" Al and I hiss together. "They'll kill us."

"Keep trying to get a signal," I tell AmberLea, "and keep GL quiet. I'm going to stall them." There's only one thing I can think of. I ditch my camera, then reach into GL's bag and pull out the can of spray paint.

Out in the clearing, Rocco Wings is saying, "It would make things a lot simpler." I palm my cell phone, still set on Bun's tattoo photo, and step out from behind the railroad ties.

"Let's make things a lot simpler right now," I say.

THIRTY-ONE

They all spin around and whip out guns; so much for being "gentlemen." All the guns are pointed at me, except maybe Rocco's. His gun is a monster revolver, so big you'd think it would tip him over, and his hand shakes so much it's hard to tell where the gun is pointed. Also, he doesn't have his giant glasses on. That's good, because it comes to me in a flash that he saw me in the TV room at Erie Estates. It doesn't help me much though. I don't care how bad the shooters are; when five guns are turned your way, you do not feel like a movie hero. But what I have to do is turn into one.

"Who the bleep are you?" shouts AB Wings. He sounds like a closet biker.

I don't say anything. Instead, I push my glasses up my nose with my cell phone hand and turn my back to them. "Drop it!" someone warns as I raise my hand, but I don't. I shake the tin of spray paint. The little ball inside it clatters like a rattlesnake. Then I spray a copy of Bunny's tattoo on the side of the boxcar.

The only sound is the hiss of the spray can. I inhale the tang of the paint. It's probably bad for you, but who cares? It might be the last thing I smell; that and insect repellent and creosote. At least I won't be around if they give me cancer. I'm trying not to imagine what it will feel like to get shot in the back, but I do anyway. Will I hear the shot before it hits me? Will I feel it or be in shock? Will I be dead before my face smacks the freight car? My back muscles are screwed so tight I can hardly lift my arm. My arm is shaking so bad I can hardly point the spray can. But there it is, white on rusty brown: a wobbly, striped number fifteen with what might be a blown-out candle beside it. I turn to the bad guys.

"You're *Posse*?" Orange Beard says. "Fifteenth Street?"

"That's right." I try to keep my voice from being as wobbly as the paint job.

"Where'd you come from?"

"Toronto. That's my car over there." I nod at the battered Civic.

"Where's Scratch?"

"Busy right now."

"Bleeping bleep bleep," says Orange Beard. He raises his gun.

"No, wait, man," says Mustache. "Scratch said they brought in this whacko little white dude. Remember?"

"That's me," I say. "Yup. I'm him." *Shut up*, I scream at myself.

"What's your name, man?"

Now I have to go with it. "Bunny."

"*Bunny*?"

"It's a nickname. You've probably got one too."

"Yeah." Mustache grins. "Meat Hook."

"Where's Scratch?" says Orange Beard, still suspicious.

"Taking care of things," I say. "There was a problem."

"No kiddin'." says Rocco Wings. "You're about ta have a bigger one. Where's my good friend Al Capoli?"

"Oh, him," I say. "Outta the picture. Not very good at cooperatin'." Why am I starting to talk like Rocco Wings? "And it's not my problem, it's yours."

"How so?" growls Rocco, waving off a blackfly. I want to do the same, but I'm scared they'll shoot if I wave my arms around.

"Point o' fact, you got two problems." I seem to be stuck with the gangster voice now. "See, he was travelin' wit' some people. One of them was our plant, my own brother. There was a girl too, underage. An' there was a good friend of yours, Mr. Wings, name of Gloria Lorraine."

For a second, Rocco Wings turns to stone on his walker seat. Then he starts shaking again, but now his eyes are glittering and his voice is more like a purr; a tiger's purr, maybe. "Where is she?"

"Not far. She's with some of our people. She's safe—for now. The others? Not so lucky. *Boom, boom, boom*. All gone."

"You zipped your own brother?" says KK Wings.

I shrug. "It's business. If he was willin' to snitch on his friends, maybe he'd rat me out someday." I don't know where this is coming from or exactly where it's going. I seem to be channeling every mobster movie I've ever seen. For now I'm going to ignore that none of them have happy endings, because I've got the beginning of an idea.

I've almost got it figured out when Mister Bones comes trotting out of the bush. I hadn't even noticed he'd gone. Now he's the sole survivor of my made-up massacre unless he trots over to Al and gives everyone else away. He yips and starts toward me, then sees the Wings and starts to growl. I do the only thing I can think of. I dig in my pocket for Al's car keys. "Mister Bones!" I call. "Mister Bones!" I jingle the keys till he looks at me. "Go get 'em!" Then I throw the keys as far as I can into the bush. As Mister Bones dashes off, I hear a noise behind me that might be Al moaning again.

"Whaddabout Miz Lorraine?" Rocco Wings says. He's got those glittering eyes locked on me now, boring into me like lasers, even without his glasses. Sweat is running under my shirt.

"With all our hearts we wanna see her back with you and safe at home," I say, "but first, see, there's this other little problem."

"What might that be?"

"It's the product. It's not classic *or* diet." Now they're all looking at me hard. If I ever get out of this,

I promise myself I'll find out what that means. In the meantime, I pray AmberLea has found a cell signal and called the cops before these guys shoot everything in sight, and that I can get everyone away from here and back to the Superior Motel before the Wings and the bikers find them. It occurs to me that throwing away the car keys probably didn't help, but it's too late now. Besides, I need time to also pray that Al really is the King of Cannoli as well as a drug-dealing gangster.

"If it isn't product, then what is it?" says Mustache.

"It's icing sugar."

"What the—?"

They all turn toward the Cadillac, except for Rocco Wings, who keeps his beady old eyes more or less on me. As they start across the gravel, I wonder if it really is icing sugar. I wonder if I can get over and grab Rocco's gun while they leave him alone. Then I wonder what I'd do with it if I had it. If I knew how to ride a motorcycle, I could jump on one of the choppers and roar off for help. Maybe I could dive into the Lincoln. In the movies, the bad guys always leave the keys in the ignition.

I don't do any of it, of course, but it doesn't matter. Before the Wings and the bikers even get to the Caddy, there are faint crashing noises from the far end of the clearing. Out of the bush stumble two black guys, waving crazily at the blackflies swarming around them. The bigger one is wearing a basketball jersey over a white T-shirt, huge hip-hop jeans, gigantic untied runners and a barrel-size silver fullback cap twisted to one side. Not to mention a lot of bling. His voice carries across the clearing. "Jackfish! Jackfish, my butt! Drive all night! Forget *classic*, there's *nothin'* there!"

The smaller guy is wearing a black dress shirt under a black suit and those dress shoes that make it look as if your toes are an extra six inches long. He looks like a hip young business guy in a bank ad. He's not saying anything. But together, Orange Beard and AB Wings say, "Hey, that's Scratch!"

Oh. No.

THIRTY-TWO

The black guys look our way when they hear voices. Then the one in the suit—Scratch, I guess—starts to jog toward us. I want to run away, but I can't make anything move.

Then I'm guessing he sees the guns and the Cadillac and he slows down near the Civic. "Glad you made it," he calls out. "That what we're looking for?"

"You should know." Mustache laughs.

"You finish your business?" That's Rocco's voice. Scratch doesn't see him at first; then he looks over. The little old gangster has shuffled his walker halfway around so he can see Scratch.

Scratch looks confused for a second; then he gives a little laugh and says, "Thought we were going to get started."

"Where's Miz Lorraine?" Rocco Wing's voice has the tiger purr in it again.

"Miss—who?"

"Your boy Bunny here says you got her for safe-keeping." Rocco shakes a hand in my general direction. "He also says the product is icing sugar. Are you saying we're pulling a double cross, or are you pulling one?"

"Bunny?" Scratch is clearly trying to catch up. "You mean the white dude? He's in—"

"Hey," says the hip-hopper. "Who tagged us on the train car?"

"Bunny," says KK, pointing to me.

"That's not Bunny, man. He's in T.O."

They all turn to look at me. Rocco Wings has put his glasses on. "I thought I seen you before," he purrs.

"I'm Spencer," I yell to Scratch. "Bunny's brother! You know, the one who told him where we were."

Rocco Wings raises his monster revolver and fires at me. The *crack* and *whang* as it ricochets off a freight car makes me almost, but not quite, wet my pants. I'm not sure which is the bigger surprise:

that I almost wet my pants, or that I manage not to. Wet pants never seem to be an issue in action movies. Not that it matters. Rocco's voice snaps me back to the real problem.

"Where's Miz Lorraine?"

And now it's all over. I don't know what else to do, except hope they've snuck away.

"She's—she's back here, behind the wood. They all are."

"Tell them to come out. I needa speak to Miz Lorraine."

Al comes out first. "Rocco," he pleads, then turns to KK. "Vincent. Check the bags. I tried to tell you. It explains everything."

Nobody says a word but Rocco, who says, "You, I do personal."

"No signal," AmberLea whispers to me, as she helps GL out from behind the railroad ties. She has my camera strap slung over her shoulder. Rocco pulls off his glasses as soon as GL appears.

"Rocco," GL cries. "What a nice surprise! What brings you up to this neck of the woods?" You have to hand it to her.

Rocco sighs. "Miz Lorraine—"

"Gloria, puhleeease."

"Miz Lorraine—Gloria—I've always been what you call a sincere admirer, more thanna fan, you know. And it's been a joy anna pleasure to, so to speak, make your acquaintance these last few years. So I want to tell you myself that I'm sorry it has to end this way. Also, I know that you was married long enough to Little Moe Chopsticks, may he rest in peace, to unnerstan that it's gotta happen."

GL nods, then tips her head up and angles her eyebrow in her classic pose. "Oh, I understand. Women were born to understand. A kiss and a kiss-off; what's the difference?"

If I had what it took to care right now, I'd ask which of her movies she took that from. It doesn't matter; she's already moved on.

"Do what you have to, but I need to do something first. You're too much of a gentleman to refuse a lady's last request, Rocco."

"As long as it don't take too long," says Rocco Wings.

"This young man"—GL waves gracefully at me—"is only here because his grandfather's dying request was that he get a kiss from me. I promised

I'd kiss him if he got me here, to the graveyard."
She gives a little laugh. "Maybe this *is* the right
ending, for me anyway. Everyone is here because
of me. I'm sorry about that. The boy's grandfather
was a good man. No matter what happens, I have
to honor his request."

"Make it snappy."

"Up yours," says Gloria Lorraine. "Spunky,
get over here."

I go over to her. "I'm sorry," I say. "I tried."

"You were sensational," she says. "David would
be so proud. Now, stand there." She moves me to
her other side, then cocks an eye up to the clouds.
"Damn, the light's bad. Never mind. Amby, set up the
shot over there. Get about three feet back. I want you
to frame it tight from a little below. Bottom it with
our shoulders. And whatever you do, no cane."
She ditches the cane and grabs me with both hands.
She's surprisingly strong.

"Got it." AmberLea hurries over and starts fussing
with the camera. "It would be better with the tripod."

"We'll make do," says GL.

"Hey, hey, wait a minute!" AB Wings starts
forward. "*VIDEO*? You can't film this!"

"Says who, you little wimp," GL snarls without looking at him. "What this boy's grandfather wants, he gets. What are you going to do, kill us?"

"Maybe I will." AB Wings checks the clip in his pistol.

Rocco Wings raises his shaky hand. "Maybe you won't; not until I say so."

AB stops and glares. His pink oxford button-down has come untucked under his blazer. He backs off, muttering.

"Think, Tiffy..." Rocco calls to AB.

Tiffy, I think to myself. I'm going to get shot by a guy named Tiffy. So much for AB.

"...It's not as if anybody's gonna see it," Rocco finishes.

"Oh, they'll see it all right," AmberLea says cheerfully, fiddling with the camera, "In fact, they're seeing it right now. They've seen everything since you got here."

"What are you bleeping talking about?" says Mustache.

AmberLea holds up a hand; her cell phone is in it. A black wire is running from the phone to the camera. "We've been Skyping the whole thing to all

Spencer's web subscribers ever since we got here. He has a lot of fans. Say hi to the nice people." She swings the camera toward the Wings and the bikers and the posse dudes. There's a lot of twisting and bleeping as hands cover faces. "It's okay," AmberLea says. "We got some good shots earlier, even your license plates. Anyway, we'd better hurry, because the cops will probably be here soon. Especially since I'm skipping out on house arrest and wearing one of these." She yanks up the cuff of her skinny jeans. There's something around her ankle.

"Ah, geez, bleep, bleep bleeping bleep," says Orange Beard.

"What is it?" says Rocco.

"It's a GPS ankle cuff, Pop," says AB Wings. "Remember when Vincent was under—"

"I remember, I remember. The cops are coming? The hell with this. Let's pop 'em now."

"Good thinking," says AmberLea. "Murder charges on top of everything else; sounds like a plan to me."

Rocco Wings isn't listening. He's fumbling with his glasses and the pistol on his knees. Behind him I hear an engine trying to start. We all look. Scratch and his homey are in the Civic.

"Bleep this," says Orange Beard, "I'm outta here." He heaves his gun as far as he can into the bush and runs for his chopper. Well, not exactly *runs*. It's hard to run in bike leathers, chains and boots, especially if you're short and four feet wide. Let's say he waddles fast. Mustache beats him to the bikes by a mile. He's trying to kick-start the bike and throw away his knife and gun all at the same time when Orange Beard gets there. The Civic engine is still trying to turn over as KK and AB grab Rocco's walker with him still in the seat and half carry, half hustle him toward the suv, his little white shoes waving in the air, the monster gun swinging wildly. Rocco gets off two shots. The first one hits a woodpile, and I guess the second one hits the helium tank in the Caddy because there's a *BOOM* and the trunk lid shoots off, and suddenly white powder is wafting down on the whole clearing. It makes a nice, Christmas-style ending as four Ontario Provincial Police cruisers roll into the clearing, roof lights whirling.

For a second the whole scene looks as if it's frozen inside one of those snow-globe shakers. Then I look at AmberLea and stammer, "How…? Did you…? Were they…? Is that really…?"

AmberLea shakes her head. She lifts her phone and the camera. The wire for her earbuds runs from the phone to the bottom of the video cam. It's stuck there with a piece of gum. AmberLea is a criminal genius.

"To hell with that," says Gloria Lorraine. "It was a beautiful scene, Amby. You played it like a pro. I wish we'd worked together more. Now, get me to the graveyard." She tugs at my arm to steady herself and goes down like a house of cards.

THIRTY-THREE

Jer and Mike Karpuski and a lady who turns out to be AmberLea's mom, Tina, arrive just before the ambulance does. Mike tells us he called the cops. "I parked at the top of Jackfish Road after you turned," he says into the camera. "I was going to cruise down in a bit and make sure everything was okay when the bikers and the suv all headed down there too, and that seemed kind of funny, so I called the plates in to the guys at the OPP detachment here. It turned out they were very interested."

The staticky chatter of police radios washes over everything. Scratch and his homey are already in the back of a cruiser; Mustache and Orange Beard are being loaded into two separate ones. Al and the Wings are in a line, handcuffed, by the suv. The rain of white powder has left them looking as if they all have really bad dandruff. KK keeps running a finger across the shoulder of his brother's blazer, and then licking off the powder. "It really is icing sugar," he keeps saying.

"I tried to tell ya," Al says sadly. "The delivery guy never showed with the merchandise. That was supplies for the bakery."

"Alphonso." Rocco Wings looks up from where he's cuffed to the seat of his walker. "On behalf 'a my boys, I apologize. It was their mistake. They're young an' hot-headed. It's the delivery guy needs a one-way ticket, maybe. But lissen, it was business, nothin' personal. I will square it with you by picking up the lawyers on this one."

"Accepted. I unnerstan, Rocco; I got kids of my own. I'm honored to take your offer. I'll send a special cake for your birthday."

Rocco Wings nods, then glares at his boys. "Kids these days," he says.

"Tell me about it," Al says, as Mister Bones comes trotting over, the car keys jingling in his mouth.

Jer is standing by himself in the middle of the clearing, arms crossed, slowly looking things over. He's wearing the same clothes he had on in Buffalo, except he's added a too-long flannel shirt. Orange plaid. I know it's not his, but I've seen it before.

"How've you been?" he asks.

"Fine," I say. "Good."

"Glad to hear it. Looks as if I missed some fun."

"Not exactly."

We look at each other.

"Thanks for being cool with Mom," I say. "I mean, covering for me."

"That's okay, this once. We're going to have to get our story straight on the way home though."

"Sure."

I stuff my hands in my pockets. One pocket is kind of damp. Maybe I did wet myself a little. I pull my hands out.

"Uh, sorry I didn't tell you where I was going. First I didn't know, and then—I dunno—I just had to do it."

"I understand."

I look at him. By now my glasses are so bent I can only see out of one lens. Jer is a little fuzzy around the edges, but the middle of him is clear and sharp.

"I'll tell you about it," I say. "You should hear first."

"When you're ready," he says.

Then I think of something else.

"So, uh, what did *you* do for three days?" I ask.

Jer looks at me for a long time. "First I freaked out," he says. "Then I ran into Erie Estates and they freaked out and called Tina. When Tina arrived, we all freaked out. And then I decided to do what you asked."

"Huh?"

"Trust you." He hugs me really hard. I hug him back.

Jer says, "I went someplace quiet and did some thinking. There were some things I needed to work out. I've ditched the novel, for one. Anyway, I'll tell you later. You set a good example, kid."

The ambulance is pulling in. "I'll be right back," I say to Jer. As the ambulance and I crunch across the gravel, I remember where I've seen the shirt. At the cottage. Grandpa would wear it on cool days. He called it his go-to-hell shirt. I guess Jer will tell me about it, when he's ready.

GL is still on the ground. AmberLea and her mom, Tina, are crouching beside her. They've gotten her partly wrapped up in a blanket, and a coat is folded up under her head.

"…and then my leg just went out from under me," GL is saying. Her face is pale. I notice for the first time that she's not wearing much makeup this morning.

"I know, Mother. You've told us. It happens some-times with older people. I just wish you'd told us what you wanted. I'd have—"

"I wanted," says GL, "to share this with AmberLea, before she turned into me, doing wild, stupid things."

"You could have shared it with me too," says Tina. "I don't even know what we're doing up here."

"I thought it was too late for that," says GL. She's biting at her lips. "I wasn't much of a mother. I never even told you who I was. And then Amby getting into trouble…I thought at least with that ankle gizmo you'd know where she was."

"The—oh, good god, that thing doesn't really work. They just put it on to scare some sense into her. I've been frantic. If Mr. O'Toole hadn't called me…"

"Doesn't work?" says AmberLea. "You're kidding!"

Doesn't work? I think, remembering all those guns. I almost fall down myself.

"It's not too late, Gramma," says AmberLea. She's holding GL's hand, at least until the paramedics ask her to stand back. They swing a stretcher down into position, all calm talk and asking questions about what happened and where it hurts. GL winces and yelps when they lift her onto the stretcher. The ground is rough, so they carry it instead of using the wheels. As the paramedics lift her into the ambulance she spots me. "Spencer," she says. "Like Spencer Tracey. That's how I remember it. You've been a good sport, Spencer. Come here. In here. AmberLea!" she calls. "Bring the camera."

I climb in and kneel beside her. "Lose the glasses," she orders. "Prop up this pillow. More. There. You," she says to a paramedic, "get a flashlight. We need a small spot."

"Ma'am—" the paramedic starts to say.

"Just do it, we haven't got all day. No wonder pictures go over budget."

AmberLea sets up the shot for GL's good side. GL directs the lighting. "How's my hair? All right. Spencer, turn the other way; we shoot faces, not ears."

I bend in. This close she's a very old, very pale lady and her lips are quivering with pain. She reaches out a hand that's all bones and blue veins and red polish. I understand and reach my hand out to her. Her hand is cool. It clutches tight. She pulls me in close for the shot. "I meant everything I said out there," she whispers. Her breath is like a musty sweater. Then, louder, "All right," she says, "this is for David McLean, from Wanda Karpuski." She kisses me on the cheek.

I start to get up and she pulls me back. "And this is for Spencer, from Gloria Lorraine." She kisses me again.

"Cut," says AmberLea.

REEL FOUR

BLACK SCREEN

SOUND OF HELICOPTER

FADE IN:

EXT.—HIGHWAY 17 AERIAL SHOT—DAY

Chopper swoops low and follows Jackfish Road. Fall colors dot the landscape. To the south, the gray-blue swell of Lake Superior.

EXT.—CLEARING LONG SHOT, FROM GROUND—DAY

Chopper lands in clearing. TINA, AMBERLEA, JERRY, DEB and MIKE KARPUSKI climb out. SPENCER is not in the group. JERRY carries a shovel, TINA a bag.

EXT.—FOREST HAND—HELD TRAVELING SHOT GROUP, FROM BEHIND—DAY

Group walks through forest along railroad tracks. They turn off into a small clearing, almost over-grown, with wire fencing around.

SOUND OF FEET CRUNCHING.

TINA

It's too bad your son Bunny can't be here.

DEB

Thanks. I know he wishes he could.

JERRY

Yeah. At least he'll be out in less than a year.

EXT.—GRAVEYARD MEDIUM SHOT GROUP—DAY

TINA, AMBERLEA, JERRY, DEB and MIKE KARPUSKI are in graveyard. Red and orange leaves blaze as sunlight filters through the trees. One wooden cross still leans against wire fence, one has fallen over.

SOUND OF MURMURING VOICES, WIND RUSTLES
LEAVES. A LAST FEW INSECTS BUZZ.

CLOSE-UP OF WRITING ON STANDING CROSS
Writing is in a strange language, maybe Latin.

CLOSE-UP OF WRITING ON FALLEN CROSS
Writing is too faint to read.

                    MIKE (OFFSCREEN)
        Here.

PAN TO:
MEDIUM SHOT—MIKE
MIKE points to the earth at his feet. It has sunk
a little. A dead tree has fallen across it and there's a
piece of rotten wood at one end, like the wood of
the crosses.

MIKE lifts away the log and clears the space.

JERRY digs a small hole near the rotten wood.

TWO SHOT—TINA AND AMBERLEA

TINA and AMBERLEA are holding a round metal box.
(The kind used to hold a reel of movie film.)
TINA opens it.

AMBERLEA wears a small antique locket hanging
over her sweater.

CLOSE-UP—AMBERLEA'S AND TINA'S HANDS

AMBERLEA and TINA put a copy of the picture of
Danielle and one of Gloria as a movie star in the box.
AMBERLEA opens the locket to show the original
picture of Danielle. She closes the locket. They close
the box.

MEDIUM SHOT—ALL

TINA and AMBERLEA put the box in the hole and
step back. JERRY fills in the hole. Then DEB hangs a
small circular object on a loop of rawhide to the wire
fence behind.

**CLOSE-UP—ONE OF GRANDPA'S AIR FORCE IDENTITY
DISCS**

MEDIUM SHOT—ALL

Everyone bows their heads; then everyone hugs.

SOUND OF VOICES, BREEZE, ETC.

AMBERLEA walks toward, then off camera.

SOUND OF HER FEET CRUNCHING ON LEAVES
CLOSE BY.

SOUND STOPS.

            AMBERLEA (OFFSCREEN)
    You know, Spencer, this could be the start of
    a beautiful friendship…

TILT UP FROM GROUP TO EXTREME WIDE SHOT—
CLEAR BLUE SKY

A jet's vapor trail cuts across the sky.

SONG FROM CASABLANCA, "AS TIME GOES BY"

FADE TO BLACK

ACKNOWLEDGMENTS

There are a whole bunch of people who deserve most of the credit and none of the blame for this book.

First, my thanks to Eric Walters, who dreamed up Grandpa David and the whole Seven series, for both a great idea and his generosity in inviting me along for the ride. Also, thanks to Richard Scrimger. It was fun dreaming up Spencer and Bunny's family and coordinating their adventures.

Peter Carver kindly gave me the tablecloth trick. As well, I'm indebted to Pat Devereaux and Mike Glover, who pointed me toward Jackfish. My old buddy Frank Rolfe made sure I got the details of his cottage right by inviting me up to visit; I'm grateful.

I'd also like to thank the folks at Orca for their support of this project, especially editor extraordinaire Sarah Harvey, who kept a firm hand on the steering wheel whenever Spencer's story started to careen out of control.

Finally, my gratitude to Margaret and to Will for great advice and for being there.

When he isn't writing, TED STAUNTON has a busy schedule as a speaker, workshop leader, storyteller and musical performer for children and adults. His previous books include the well-loved Green Applestreet Gang series, as well as *Hope Springs a Leak* and *Power Chord*. Ted lives in Port Hope, Ontario. To learn more about Ted, go to www.tedstauntonbooks.com.

SEVEN
THE SERIES

7 GRANDSONS
7 JOURNEYS
7 AUTHORS
1 AMAZING SERIES